Note to Readers

Although the Lankford and Miller families are fictional, other characters you will meet in *Earthquake in Cincinnati* are not. Dr. Drake, Mr. and Mrs. Roosevelt, and even the big dog, Tiger, actually lived. The earthquake and aftershocks that are described in this book happened too, as did the strange migration. And yes, for a short time, the force of the earthquake caused the Mississippi River to flow backward. Small aftershocks were felt for two years after the quake.

The burns that are described in *Earthquake in Cincinnati* were all too common in the early 1800s. Because houses were heated by fires in unscreened fireplaces and food was cooked in huge kitchen fireplaces, it was much easier for sparks to fly out and start a house fire or catch someone's clothes on fire. Kettles sometimes tipped off the cranes that held them over the fire, and the hot food they held would spill on nearby women and children. Being burned was one of the leading causes of death at that time.

Not only are serious burns less common today than they were almost two hundred years ago, but the way we treat them has changed, too. While plunging a fresh burn into cold water is recommended, putting lard, butter, or any other type of fat on it will only make fresh burns worse.

The American Adventure

EARTHQUAKE
in
CINCINNATI

Bonnie Hinman

BARBOUR
PUBLISHING, INC.
Uhrichsville, Ohio

To my family—Bill, Beth, and Brad—with love

© MCMXCVII by Barbour Publishing, Inc.

ISBN 1-57748-231-X

Published by Barbour Publishing, Inc., P.O. Box 719, Uhrichsville, Ohio 44683
http://www.barbourbooks.com

ecpa Member of the
Evangelical Christian
Publishers Association

Printed in the United States of America.

Cover illustration by Peter Pagano.
Inside illustrations by Adam Wallenta.

CHAPTER ONE

Surprise on the River

George heard the sound first. It wasn't loud, but it was persistent and different from any sound he'd heard before. He stopped right in the middle of the dirt street to listen. What was that sound?

His plan to head for the creek to take a quick look for frogs before doing his chores was forgotten. He tilted his head and slowly turned. The noise was coming from the direction of the river. And it was getting louder. There was no decision to be made. George stashed his frog bucket under a bush by the road and ran toward the riverfront.

In the minute it took George to run the short distance to

the water, other people had also begun to take notice of the noise and move toward the docks that lined the shore of the Ohio River as it flowed past Cincinnati. George didn't stop to ask anyone what was happening. Better to find out for himself. Besides, they all looked as puzzled as he was by the sound that was fast becoming downright noisy.

George skidded to a stop, leaving a cloud of dust in his wake, and darted through the growing crowd to the water's edge. He scanned the broad river. There was some kind of boat upstream. Was the noise coming from it?

He climbed on a barrel that was waiting to be loaded onto a nearby keelboat. His blue eyes strained toward the craft. Was something wrong with the boat? Smoke and sparks flew from a tall, round chimney. Maybe the boat was on fire. But the chimney itself didn't appear to be burning. What was causing all that smoke?

More and more people hurried down the streets to the waterfront. Even their excited voices couldn't drown out the noise coming from the boat as it drew ever closer to the docks. George felt his heart race. Whatever the boat was, it was going to land. He would be able to get a good look at it.

Someone in the back of the crowd yelled, "Steamboat! It's a steamboat!"

George almost toppled off the barrel. A steamboat! He had never seen one, but he had heard of them. The newspapers said that a steamboat could go upstream without sails to power it or men to pole it through the water. Somehow steam was used to make big paddles turn in the water and pull the ship against the current.

Steamboats didn't have to wait for favorable winds to make progress up a river, and using a steam engine took a lot less work and was a lot faster than having a group of men pole a boat upstream. At least that was what his father said was the advantage of steamboats. George's father was a ship-builder himself, so he should know. But his father had only talked about the steamboats that ran on the rivers back East. What was one doing here in Cincinnati?

George hopped down off the barrel. The boat was approaching slowly, whatever its method of power. Maybe he could find his father and see if he knew any more about this noisy, spark-spitting, smoke-belching ship.

As it turned out, his father was almost right behind him. Father stood with several men who worked with him in his boatyard. George quickly scanned the faces of the workers. Evidently work had stopped for the time being, because everyone who worked in the boatyard was out watching the steamboat. No one wanted to miss the excitement, especially if they made a living building boats.

"Is it really a steamboat?" George asked, racing up to his father. "What's it doing here? I thought steamboats only ran in the East."

"Whoa, boy. Take it easy." George's father pulled him out of the way of a very large woman who was trying to squeeze closer to the dock. "Yes, it's a steamboat. Quite the noisy little vessel, isn't she?"

"And smoky too," George added. "But why here?" he asked again. At the same time he tried to look out at the water to see if the boat was closer. It sounded like it was, but the

7

large lady was definitely blocking his view.

"I'm getting to that," Father said in answer to George's question. "We've heard stories for months from the boatmen that a steamboat was under construction at Pittsburgh, but we didn't have any way of confirming that the stories were true. Then this morning two different keelboats came in, telling the tale of how they had passed up the fancy steamboat."

Father grinned at the other men standing with him. "My guess is that the steamboat was tied up at a landing taking on wood when the keelboats won that race. You have to expect a keelboat man to exaggerate a little for the sake of the story."

"Why didn't you tell me?" George was still trying to see around the woman.

"Well, now, that might be because I haven't seen hide nor hair of you all day, son. Not even to do your Saturday work with the men and me." George's father gave his son a pointed look.

George looked anywhere but at his father. He knew Father's brown eyes didn't miss much. "I was just getting ready to come," George said.

He was saved from any further explanation by the sudden scream of a whistle. It could only have come from the steamboat. "I'm going back to my barrel," he called to his father as he turned in that direction. "Better view there."

Glancing up just long enough to make sure his father had heard him over the sound of the steamboat, George pushed his way back to the barrel and sat on top of it to watch the boat as it approached the water's edge. He'd find out more from his father later. There was no need to draw attention to his absence from the boatyard this morning.

George had been sticking close to home the last few days, hoping to avoid certain situations and people, not to avoid work, as his father had suggested. And the whole scheme was turning out to be downright troublesome. If his father heard George's explanation, he would say that there was nothing for George to be hiding from. His father would be wrong.

There was another shriek from the boat's whistle. George stood up again. The boat was close enough now so that he could see people on the decks and what looked like a huge dog. George had a lot of faith in a dog's ability to size up a situation. It was hard to tell the dog's state of mind from shore, but he appeared calm. George judged this to be a good sign. Perhaps the boat wasn't in such immediate danger of blowing up as the sparks and smoke and noise seemed to indicate.

"George, scoot over."

George looked down to see his cousin Betsy standing by the barrel. At seventeen, Betsy was two and a half years older than George and one of his best friends, although he wouldn't be likely to admit that to any of the boys at school. He and Betsy had traveled together to Cincinnati with their families all the way from Boston a few years ago. When he was younger, tormenting Betsy had been a favorite pastime. But after their trip together from Boston, all that had changed. He still teased her a little sometimes, but not at all like before.

"Come on up," George invited, brushing his straight blond hair out of his eyes. He moved over, making a few more inches of room, and brushed some dirt off.

Betsy frowned as she looked at the top of the barrel.

9

"Maybe not. There's not much room. We'd probably fall off and roll into the Ohio."

"At least you can sit on the edge," George offered. "I'd be happy to stand behind you."

"Thanks, but I'll just stand beside you." She looked out across the river. "I can see everything from here. Being tall helps in this instance."

George sat down again on the barrel top. Betsy didn't seem as tall as she used to. Her unusual height had been what he teased her about the most. He watched her for a moment as she stared out at the river. He knew she often came to the docks to watch the boats come in. When he asked her why once, she had just shaken her head and said she was watching for Richard.

Her cousin Richard Allerton had been forced into the British navy years ago, before they'd moved from Boston. George thought it nigh on to impossible that Richard would show up in Boston again, much less Cincinnati, but he didn't say that to Betsy. He couldn't see the sense in telling her something he couldn't prove and knew would only make her sad.

"It looks like it's going to blow up," Betsy said. "It wouldn't, would it?" She shaded her green eyes and stared out at the boat.

"Blow up!" George repeated. "I wouldn't think so." He chuckled briefly. "They've got a dog on that boat. Nobody would take a dog on board if it wasn't safe."

Betsy slowly shook her head. "You and dogs. I've noticed that not everyone likes dogs as much as you do. By the way, how is that mangy old mutt of yours? I haven't seen him around lately. Is he still pestering your neighbors?"

"Jefferson is just fine, thank you." George ignored Betsy's jab. He knew that she liked Jefferson as well as she was likely to care for any dog, in spite of the fact that at one time Jefferson had seemed bent on destroying everything she owned.

"In fact, where have you been lately?" Betsy twisted around to look George in the eye. "You're usually positively underfoot with your inventions and experiments and observations. But this week I haven't seen you at all until today."

Betsy raised her eyebrows as she tilted her head and looked at George.

"Oh, don't give me that look. I've been busy. That's all." He stood back up on top of the barrel. Busy staying out of sight. Busy not getting underfoot. Busy avoiding someone. Busy in this case meant boring. He glanced down at Betsy's brown head. He'd like to tell her all about his problems, but somehow he didn't think she'd understand. He had a feeling he knew what she'd say, and it wasn't what he wanted to hear. Better to just keep quiet and wait the whole mess out. He'd been praying about it, but God had been quiet, too, as far as George could tell.

That was something else that puzzled George. He couldn't seem to tell when God was telling him something and when it was his own brain doing the talking. How did a person figure that out, anyway?

"George, look!" Betsy pointed at the steamboat. It was much closer. "There's a woman on board."

Others in the crowd saw the woman also, and excited voices rose briefly over the clanking and clattering noise that

11

threatened to deafen them all. George saw that the woman stood near the bow of the boat with the big dog beside her. She was waving at the people on shore. Now George could see the name of the steamboat where it was painted on the side: the *New Orleans*.

Suddenly the crowd surged forward, and George's barrel began to tilt. He tried to catch his balance, but there wasn't anything to hold onto. He braced himself to go flying and land on the dock or maybe get dunked in the river. But someone managed to grab his arm in the confusion and yank hard.

George found himself in one piece on his feet, watching the barrel roll into the Ohio with a mighty splash. Rubbing a now-sore shoulder, he looked up at his rescuer.

It was Andrew Farley. He was the son of a local farmer and several years older than George. George didn't really know Andrew, although they did attend the same church. Lately it just seemed like Andrew had been around all the time. Especially if Betsy was nearby.

"Andrew, thank you so much," Betsy said. "George could have been killed if you hadn't saved him."

George opened his mouth to protest. After all it was just a barrel, not the top of a barn. Then he saw Betsy's face as she smiled up at Andrew. And she was smiling up, because Andrew was very big.

George stifled a groan. He wanted to yell at Betsy to stop smiling all moony at that farmer, but he didn't. Instead he simply thanked his rescuer and turned his back on the couple so he wouldn't have to see the sickening way Andrew stared down at Betsy's curly brown hair.

Anyway, the *New Orleans* was practically upon them. Sparks flew and smoke poured from the round chimney. George judged the boat to be over a hundred feet long and maybe twenty-five feet wide. It sat deeper in the water than a keelboat and had round wheels with paddles on either side. George knew from listening to his father and the other men that the paddle wheels were what propelled the boat.

The steam engine had to be below deck in the hull, George figured, because he couldn't see it, although the dock was practically vibrating from the noise it created. Several ladies in the crowd were covering their ears at the sound, and some babies were crying in protest.

A large cabin covered a good portion of the deck of the *New Orleans*. There were also two tall masts for sailing. George grinned at this. Evidently the captain was taking no chances on being left without some form of power.

Another blast of the whistle sounded, followed by a loud hissing. The crowd's gasp could be heard over the noise. There was a clanking sound, and then the engine noise got noticeably quieter, although it was still plenty loud. George looked for a way to get closer. The *New Orleans* was preparing to come about and tie up at the dock. He didn't want to miss a minute of this event.

"George, wait." Betsy's voice in his ear stopped him.

"I want to get closer." George turned impatiently toward his cousin.

"Just wait until it stops. Please?" Betsy still stood beside Andrew, but all her attention was on George.

George huffed out his frustration. "Oh, all right. But just for a minute. I want to see that engine."

"What?" Betsy called.

"Just for a minute," George repeated, raising his voice. "I want to see that engine." He pointed toward the boat and moved back a couple steps. Betsy was always trying to slow him down. He tried not to think about how often she had been right when she'd told him to wait. Just because she was right didn't mean he had to like it.

"What makes that thing go?" Andrew asked as the trio stood together watching the crew tie up the boat.

"Well, it's steam," George replied, surprised to notice that he didn't have to yell to be heard. The noise was steadily decreasing. "It has a steam engine. My father said that steam causes the parts of the engine to move." He looked thoughtful. "I wonder how it does that."

"Water expands when it turns to steam." The answer came from a voice behind George.

"Of course!" George exclaimed. For a split second, the simple explanation and its significance filled his mind. But in the next second he realized that he knew who the voice with the answer belonged to. And that realization made him forget about steam and engines and boats.

He whirled around to look into the red puckered face of Charles Lidell. Charles was the reason that the last week had been such a trial for George. The reason he had been hiding out. The reason George now wished he had fallen off the barrel and into the Ohio. Floating with the fish would be better than this.

CHAPTER TWO
The Steamboat

Irritation welled up in George, but he dropped his head and mumbled a hello to Charles. He slowly turned his body and tried to take a sneaky look around to see if anyone he knew was standing nearby. He didn't see the Jackson brothers or anyone else from school for that matter. That was a relief.

With a deep breath he straightened up and gave Charles a feeble grin before looking back at the activity on the dock in front of them. He saw a questioning frown on Betsy's freckled face as he turned away. He knew what that look meant, too: Why aren't you being friendly to the new boy?

George had a perfectly good answer, but he was thankful he didn't have to give it to his cousin right now. She had an annoying way of making perfectly good answers seem wrong. And he was in no mood to have to argue his case with anyone, least of all Betsy.

"So that's how it works," said Andrew, who was crowded up next to Betsy. "The water expands into steam and drives the engine parts."

"Sort of," said Charles. "The steam goes from the boilers to the engine, where it condenses and makes a vacuum that drives the pistons, which turn the two paddle wheels."

Andrew laughed. "If you say so. But it doesn't seem like steam could be powerful enough to drive a boat like that."

"They say it will go against the current, too," Charles said.

"Is that right?" Andrew just shook his head. "Doesn't seem likely, somehow."

"Are you Charles Lidell?" Betsy asked.

"Yes. I just moved here," Charles answered with a grin.

George was watching out of the corner of his eye and saw Betsy's face light up in pleasure. He felt like groaning. First Andrew paid too much attention to Betsy and was still standing way too close to her in George's opinion. Now Charles was grinning at her, and Betsy looked like meeting Charles was the best thing that had happened to her in weeks. What was it with these people?

"Your parents own the new mercantile near George's house, don't they?" At Charles's nod, Betsy continued. "I was in there just yesterday. It's a wonderful store and such a good location for it. I think our parents have met, too. My father is Dr. Miller. I'm Betsy, George's cousin, and this is Andrew Farley. How did you like your trip out here, and where did you move from?"

Charles chuckled and said, "Let's just say I'm glad the move is over. We came out from New York State. There were lots of interesting things to see, but the trip was long and there's something nice about sleeping on your own bed again, especially when there isn't a river moving under it."

"I know just what you mean," Betsy said. "I don't think I'll ever forget the trip George and I made out here with our parents. Someone tried to rob us, I almost drowned, and then when we finally arrived in Cincinnati, the warehouse where we were storing our things got flooded by the river. Fortunately we managed to get everything to higher ground before the waters reached the warehouse. But we almost lost George's dog, Jefferson, in the flood."

"That must have been some welcome to your new home," Charles commented. "At least we didn't have to deal with robbers or bad weather. Did you ever wish you had stayed back in Boston?"

George listened attentively to the conversation while pretending to watch the *New Orleans*. Finally he couldn't help himself and turned around to look at Betsy in amazement. Shy Betsy seldom talked to people she didn't know well, and she never struck up conversations with strangers. Here she was chattering away to a person she'd never met as if it were the most natural thing in the world. And Charles wasn't just any stranger at that.

George could say it to himself, even if he never said it aloud. Charles looked like some kind of freak. George could admit that the boy's dark hair and brown eyes were normal enough. And there was nothing unusual about his height or build. But the first thing anyone noticed about Charles was the bright red puckered scars that covered his face and hands.

It wasn't that George didn't feel sorry for Charles, because he knew that the awful scars weren't the other boy's fault. George's mother had told him that Charles had been scalded when he'd accidentally pulled a pot of boiling water over onto himself when he was four. It wasn't the scars, George had decided, that had kept him hiding this week, trying to avoid Charles's friendly approaches.

He glanced at the others again as they laughed and talked. He wasn't put off by Charles's scars. He just didn't need another friend. He had plenty of good friends already. Why, he really had no time to spend with Charles. This new boy would be better off finding someone else to be his friend, and George was doing him a favor by not encouraging him to pursue a friendship.

Just then there was finally some movement down at the water's edge. A plank clattered into place to bridge the gap from boat to dock. George put his troubles aside as he tried to stretch up and peer over the people who had pushed in front of him. It looked like some men were getting ready to go on board the *New Orleans*. The boat sat quietly now, with only an occasional leftover whisper of a hiss. George started trying to figure out how he could get on board the new boat.

"Betsy! Betsy, over here."

George turned briefly to see who was hailing his cousin. It was Emily Stover, Betsy's best friend. The two girls had been inseparable friends ever since they had met shortly after the Stovers had arrived in Cincinnati three years ago.

Emily towed two little boys, one on each hand, and pushed her way through the crush of spectators toward Betsy. Emily's family was large, and she was seldom seen without one or two younger brothers or sisters hanging on her skirts or tugging at her arms. Not that Emily seemed to mind or even to notice most of the time.

"Isn't this just too exciting for words?" Emily pulled her charges up short before they could lunge on into the crowd. She gave a quick look at Andrew and then barely raised her eyebrows as she looked at Betsy.

Betsy's cheeks turned so pink they almost hid her freckles, but she ignored Emily's unspoken question about Andrew. "Yes, it is exciting."

"Papa is supposed to be down here somewhere." Emily scanned the crowd. "I was hoping to hand these two off to him." She yanked one of the little boys back from his investigation of the boots of a gentleman who was standing in front of them.

"I can take one of them," Betsy offered and held out her hand.

"Oh, no," Emily said as she pulled the other boy back to her side also. "Thank you for the offer, but you don't deserve that. These two are full of mischief, and I know all these rascals' tricks. Besides, Papa said he'd take them to see the boat."

19

"There's Mr. Stover over there," Andrew said, pointing toward the steamboat. "Down by the plank. It looks like he's with the mayor."

George saw that Mr. Stover was indeed standing with the mayor and a couple other townspeople. They were talking to the man George had seen on the deck of the *New Orleans*.

"That's Papa," Emily said. "He always manages to be in the middle of things. Come on boys. Let's find Papa." She tightened her grip on her younger brothers and started through the crowd, then stopped short. "Why don't you all come with us? Maybe Papa's talking to someone from the boat. Someone we might like to meet."

George didn't hesitate. He fell in right behind Emily and her brothers. "Great idea, Em."

Emily laughed. "You just behave yourself, George Lankford. Come on, the rest of you. Betsy, come on. Bring Andrew, and this is Charles, isn't it?"

"Yes, but I'm not sure if we should go." Betsy frowned. "It might be dangerous."

"I'll come with you, Betsy," Andrew said and put his hand at her elbow. "I think it's probably safe to go closer."

"Oh well, if you say so, Andrew." Betsy smiled up at the tall young man and allowed him to guide her through the crowd. "You come too, Charles," she called over her shoulder.

Charles smiled at her and quickly fell into step with the constantly increasing group.

George rolled his eyes and turned to march after Emily. This Andrew thing was downright disgusting. Not to mention that Betsy had made sure Charles came along, too.

The crowd had begun to mill around near the dock, now that they had determined nothing exciting or disastrous was likely to happen any time soon. Some of the people were heading back to their shops and homes. That made it easier for Emily and her parade of friends to reach Mr. Stover and the other gentlemen.

"Emily, my girl," Mr. Stover called. "You've brought the lads and your friends, too, I see." He smiled and waved them closer. "Come and meet Mr. Roosevelt. He's the captain of this fine steamboat."

George stepped right up. The man Mr. Stover was standing next to was tall and distinguished looking. George could have pegged him as an easterner right away. There was just something about him—maybe it was his clothes, which appeared more expensive than those worn by any ship captain George had ever seen since he left Boston. In Boston, his father had worked at the family shipyard designing big sea-going vessels, and George had grown up around ship captains.

Of course, George had never seen a steamboat captain before, let alone been introduced to him. Which is what Mr. Stover was doing. George shook hands with Mr. Roosevelt and studied him closely as the others were introduced.

"What do you think of my ship?" Mr. Roosevelt's voice boomed over George. The captain turned and waved expansively at the *New Orleans*. "Quite a marvel, isn't she? Perhaps you'd like to come aboard and see the machinery?"

"Yes, sir." George answered so quickly that the others laughed. He grinned sheepishly, and his face flushed.

"Never mind, boy," said Mr. Roosevelt. "I like a person

who knows his own mind and isn't afraid to speak up. Come along, and bring your friends."

The captain took the plank in two big steps and was talking even as he stepped lightly on the deck of the ship. Mr. Stover and the mayor followed.

George hurried after the men, calling to the others as he went. "Come on, Betsy, Andrew. Let's look."

"George, wait," Betsy said. "I don't know if this is such a good idea. I don't really want to. . ."

Her words were lost to George, but he did stop and wait after he jumped off the plank onto the deck. He saw Andrew duck his head and say something to Betsy. She raised her face toward the young man and smiled that moony smile that George had already come to hate.

"We'll stay here for now, George. Charles can go with you." Betsy motioned at Charles to go ahead, but he seemed to be waiting for some invitation from George.

"Don't wait for me," Emily yelled. "I'm not taking these two on a boat." She pulled one of her brothers back from the water's edge.

George stood where he was for a moment. He was stuck. There was no way to politely get rid of Charles, and the longer he stood hesitating, the more he was missing. Mr. Roosevelt was already talking to the mayor and Mr. Stover. He shrugged. "Come on, Charles. We don't want to miss anything."

Charles grinned and scrambled across the plank to join George.

CHAPTER THREE
Trouble with the Jacksons

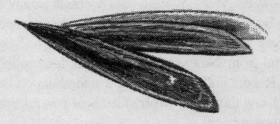

By the time George and Charles reached the group of men on the *New Orleans,* Mr. Roosevelt was talking a mile a minute as he enthusiastically described the workings of his boat. He pointed out the paddle wheels on the side and the pilot house on top. He took his visitors right down into the engine room and showed them the firebox and the boiler. He described how the steam was condensed in the boiler, and how it drove the pistons in the engine. George was fascinated, but it all seemed so complicated.

"Sir, is this a low-pressure engine?" Charles asked when Mr. Roosevelt paused for breath.

"Yes, lad. It certainly is. I feel it can get the job done with less risk than you'd have with a higher-pressure engine." The captain smiled at Charles as if pleased with his question. George wished he knew enough about steam engines to ask something intelligent.

Charles nodded and leaned over to look more closely at the engine, which seemed strangely silent after its very noisy entrance at the landing.

After answering a few more questions from the gentlemen, Mr. Roosevelt led his guests back up to the deck.

"How do you know so much about steamboats, anyway?" George whispered to Charles as they trailed after Mr. Roosevelt and the other gentlemen.

"I'm from New York State," Charles replied. "That's where Robert Fulton is running a steamboat on the Hudson River. I saw the North River steamboat several times. I even went aboard once."

"Was it like this boat?" George asked, glad that Mr. Roosevelt had been temporarily interrupted by a crew member with a question. Now he could ask Charles for more information about steamboats without missing anything the captain might have to say.

"Some," Charles replied. "The design was similar, and I'm pretty sure the engine is the same. Mr. Fulton's boat had the same side paddle wheels. I've heard that some steamboats have one paddle wheel in the stern."

"You're right about that, sir," a lilting female voice said

from behind the two boys. "Mr. Roosevelt feels that the paddle wheels on the side give the boat more ability to maneuver and greater stability."

George turned to see a dark-haired young woman standing nearby. Her smile lit up her pretty face. It was impossible not to smile back. This must surely be the woman who had been standing on the deck as the *New Orleans* had approached the river's edge. George couldn't help but notice that she looked like she was going to have a baby very soon. He remembered well how his mother had looked two years ago right before his little sister, Lucy, had been born.

"Yes, ma'am," Charles said. "I can see how side wheels might have those advantages."

"I'm Lydia Roosevelt," the young woman said. "My husband, Mr. Roosevelt, is the captain of the *New Orleans*. But I believe you have already met him."

A huge bronze dog appeared beside Mrs. Roosevelt and carefully edged his head under her hand. "This fine animal is Tiger." She gently stroked the dog's head.

"He's a handsome dog, ma'am, and so big," George said.

"Tiger appreciates the compliment," Mrs. Roosevelt replied. "He's a Newfoundland dog, named after the country in which his breed was developed. Newfoundlands are known for their large size, and Tiger certainly matches his breed's reputation. He's also very gentle.

"Now would you boys like to see the inside of the cabins? It appears that Mr. Roosevelt has gone off to talk over some problem with the crew." She gestured toward where her husband could be seen in earnest conversation with two men.

"Yes, ma'am," George answered. It was hard to keep from sounding too excited at the prospect of seeing the inside of the boat's cabins. "That is, if it's not too much trouble."

"If it's not too much trouble," Charles echoed.

"Not at all. I enjoy showing our boat to young men who appreciate good ships and fine dogs," she said with a mischievous smile. "Come this way." Mrs. Roosevelt led the boys through a door and down a step or two. "We say that the boat has two cabins, but actually it's one big cabin divided into two parts by some folding doors. The ladies' cabin is aft—that's in the back—and the gentlemen's is forward."

George saw that the floor was carpeted and that there were looking glasses on one wall. He saw several berths along another wall with curtains around them. There were high windows that let the sunshine stream in, even though the cabin was in the hold of the boat.

"This is the ladies' cabin," Mrs. Roosevelt said, "and here is our tiniest lady." She held out her hands to a small girl who sprang up from the floor where she had been playing with some wooden bowls. Another young woman had been keeping careful watch over the little girl.

"This is our daughter, Rosetta, and her nurse, Anna Lee," Mrs. Roosevelt said in introduction. She gave the little girl a hug and then handed her back to the nurse. "Now come back through the folding doors and see the gentlemen's cabin."

George found himself grinning at Charles. Would they ever have some stories to tell Betsy when they got back to their friends!

The gentlemen's cabin was much the same as the ladies'

cabin, although it was bigger and less elegant. There were a great many berths built into the walls with curtains to shield them from visitors' eyes. A long table took up the center of the room used for meals, no doubt.

"There's no carpet in here," said Mrs. Roosevelt. "The gentlemen insist on chewing that nasty tobacco, and it stains anything it touches. Chewing tobacco is a bad habit, boys. Don't start."

"Yes, ma'am," Charles and George said at the same time.

"There are some comfortable chairs and a stove for heat and a galley for cooking." Mrs. Roosevelt's expansive wave reminded George of Mr. Roosevelt's when he had gestured with pride at the *New Orleans* earlier. "My little family finds the *New Orleans* to be as comfortable and cozy as our home in New York City." Mrs. Roosevelt shook her head briefly. "Except for the noise, of course. That's dreadful, but one gets accustomed to it eventually."

In a few minutes Mrs. Roosevelt left George and Charles on the deck while she went to greet some other visitors. The boys took another peek into the machinery room.

"I'd sure like to get a better look at that engine," George said.

"Me, too," Charles agreed. "I'd like to see how that piston is connected to the beam to drive the paddle wheels."

"Do you think we dare go down there by ourselves?" George chewed his bottom lip in concentration.

"Well," Charles said, "maybe. What could it hurt? We won't touch anything. And the captain already let us into the room."

George grinned at his neighbor and realized that he hadn't even thought about Charles's scarred face since they'd started their tour of the boat. Not that it mattered, he reminded himself. The scars on Charles's face had nothing to do with George's reluctance to spend time with him.

"George! Charles!"

George made a face. "It's Betsy hollering at us. How is it that that girl manages to interrupt me about half the time when I'm getting ready to do something interesting? It never fails!"

Charles laughed. "My mother would call that the voice of God telling me to think twice about what I was about to do. Come on, let's go tell the others about the cabins."

Reluctantly George followed Charles back across the plank to the dock. It was hard to disagree with Charles, since George's own mother would no doubt say the same thing, and then she'd go on to remind him how many times he had gotten into scrapes when he hadn't listened to that voice.

Andrew and Betsy and Emily crowded around George and Charles to hear about the elegant cabins and the machinery and the dog and the little girl. Emily's father had taken over the care of her younger brothers, so for once she could give her full attention to the conversation. It was a good thing that she could because everyone was talking at once.

Suddenly a loud voice interrupted their conversation. "If it isn't the freak-boy."

George whirled around toward the source of the rude comment. His heart sank. It was the Jackson brothers. They were twins from one of the wealthier families in Cincinnati.

Their father owned one of the mills as well as many other businesses. The twins had moved to Cincinnati just that summer. Before that they had lived with their grandfather in Pittsburgh.

George had been trying to get acquainted with them. He had found out that they were interested in experiments and inventions just like he was. George's friend Franklin said that he'd heard the brothers had a fancy laboratory in their house. George wanted to see what a fully equipped laboratory looked like, and he didn't think he'd get a better opportunity than through the Jackson brothers.

"George," Ted called loudly. "What are you doing here with freak-boy?"

"We're watching the steamboat," Emily spoke up. "What's it look like? And who are you calling a freak?" The girl's brown eyes were flashing.

"Don't get all excited." Ted held his hands up in front of him. "I was just speaking to George here about the red man." Ted gestured in Charles's direction. "Hey, George. Maybe your friend here is a real red man, an Indian."

"Hey, Ted," Freddie, the other twin, spoke up. "That's a good one." He slapped his brother on the back, and the two boys started laughing. No one else joined in.

George felt panic rising. Charles just stood there, looking calmly at the Jacksons and seemingly untroubled by their hurtful words. Emily looked ready to start swinging, but Betsy grabbed her friend's arm to keep her from doing something so unladylike. Andrew looked stern but held his tongue.

George didn't know how to get the Jacksons to move on

29

without making them mad. After all, they really weren't such a bad sort. They just liked to tease. And George wanted to see their laboratory.

"Woo, woo, woo. Give us an Indian war whoop, freak-boy," Freddie said and slapped his brother on the back again. Ted took exception to this last slap and slammed up against his brother's chest.

"Come on, guys," George interrupted, trying to distract the brothers. "Let's go look at the paddle wheels." The twins shifted their attention back to George.

"What! And leave the ladies here with this red Indian?" Ted asked.

George took a deep breath. He knew that they had gone too far. Whether or not he decided to have Charles as a friend, no one deserved to be treated like this. Just as he opened his mouth to speak, Emily's two little brothers plowed into him. Somehow they had escaped from their father's care.

For a moment all was confusion. Emily dived for the two boys before they could skid off the dock into the Ohio. She missed. With his longer arms, Andrew was able to snatch up first one and then the other runaway boy and hand them over to their sister. The little boys protested loudly the whole time.

By the time everything settled down again, the Jackson brothers had lost interest and had started back up the street behind the riverfront. George started to yell after them, but then he realized that Charles had disappeared. Sometime during the chaos, the boy had slipped into the crowd that still milled around. He was nowhere to be seen.

Without a word, George walked away from Betsy and the

others and flopped down on some bags of grain that were stacked nearby. He sat and stared out into the Ohio.

The exciting day had gone flat. He knew he should have spoken up to defend Charles, but now that he didn't have to, he just felt relieved. It was not a nice feeling.

CHAPTER FOUR
The Boat-Turning

"George, come by the boatyard after school today if you would," said his father the next Friday over their noon meal. "We've got to do a boat-turning this afternoon, and we're shorthanded as it is. I've got one man off sick and another gone to Pittsburgh."

Father snatched up his old hat and started out the door. "I may have to haul some strong arms off the street."

"I'll be there," George said around a bite of bread as he hurried to finish his meal so he'd be back to school on time. "Don't turn it without me."

He jumped up and pushed his chair in. It was only recently that he had been allowed to help turn the bulky flatboats that his father and the workers at the boatyard built. When he was younger, he had only been able to watch from a distance.

"It'll be late afternoon, son, before we're ready." Father stopped and scooped up two-year-old Lucy, who had launched herself at his legs. He raised her up high above his head until she squealed with delight and her long brown hair floated in the air.

George's mother reached for the little girl. "Come here, Lucy-love. Almost time for your nap. And you two men best be going." She held Lucy on one side and began clearing the noontime dishes from the table with the other hand. "And Paul. . ."

"Yes, dear." George's father stopped short in the doorway, and George ran right into him.

"Please be careful. Those boat-turnings always make me nervous." She frowned and shook her head. "It seems like a lot of boat to be flip-flopping around in the air."

"Just like a big flapjack, Mama," George said with a laugh.

"Well, you just see that you don't get flattened like a flapjack, George Lankford." His mother's voice was stern, but her blue eyes crinkled and she laughed when she met his startled gaze.

"We'll be careful, Ellie," Father said. "George will be well out of flattening range. Won't you, George?" He gave his son a pointed look with his piercing brown eyes.

"Yes, sir," George agreed somewhat reluctantly. Actually he had been plotting in his mind about how he could get closer than he'd managed to be the last time. He wanted to be as close as he could to the real action. How else could he understand everything that went into a boat-turning?

"Come on, George," said Father. "It's past time to go." He started toward the river, while George ran down the street in the opposite direction, toward the schoolhouse. "Oh, George," Father called after him. "Bring Franklin and Allie to turn the boat if you can. And Charles, too. He looks pretty stout. We can use any extra help you can bring."

"Yes, sir," George called back. He shook his head as he sprinted toward school. Charles again. Everyone seemed bent on throwing them together. Would it never end? Why couldn't things be like they were before the Lidells had landed in Cincinnati?

The October afternoon seemed endless as George sat through arithmetic and geography classes. By the time spelling practice rolled around, George was staring out the window between writing every word on his slate. Thank goodness Mr. Simpson was grading tests. Otherwise George knew that his teacher would be roaming the schoolroom, and George's daydreaming would not escape his teacher's notice.

Not that George thought of it as daydreaming. It was thinking time, pure and simple. A man had to think sometimes. George loved all things new, but boats especially fascinated him. This steam engine was quite a development.

George stopped writing altogether. He sat with his head resting on his hand and stared at the red leaves of the maple tree that grew in the schoolyard.

The *New Orleans* had been going down the Ohio toward Louisville for three days now, and George still couldn't stop thinking about it. He'd joined hundreds of people at the docks to watch the steamboat leave. Mrs. Roosevelt, holding her daughter, Rosetta, had stood at the end of the deck, waving good-bye to the people.

It looked to George as if the big bronze Newfoundland, Tiger, was standing guard over the mother and daughter, protecting them from any danger. George wished that he could see the Roosevelts and the *New Orleans* again, because he had figured out some questions that he wanted to ask Mr. Roosevelt. But the ship was gone, heading toward the Mississippi River and eventually to the city of New Orleans.

George shook his head gently. The steamboat's visit would probably be the only excitement around Cincinnati for months to come. At least he had the boat-turning to look forward to. If only the school day would come to a close. The stuffy air in the classroom made him drowsy. His eyelids half closed.

"Mr. Lankford!"

George's head snapped up, and he quickly straightened his back. "Yes, sir," he said breathlessly.

"How fortunate for you that it's time for school to be let out," said Mr. Simpson. "Now your body can follow your mind outdoors."

There was soft laughter from the other students, but it

was soon lost in the sounds of slates being shoved in desks and feet scuffing against the wooden floorboards.

"Yes, sir," George said and quickly put away his work. He ventured a look at Mr. Simpson and was relieved to see that the teacher wasn't frowning. At least his parents wouldn't be hearing a bad report from the schoolmaster.

Once most of the students had already left the building, George hurried out the schoolhouse door and headed toward the boatyard. A quick glance around reassured him that Charles was nowhere to be seen.

The late afternoon was warm and sunny as George raced alone toward his father's business. He'd discussed the boat-turning with Franklin and Allie during the afternoon break. Both boys had to go straight home after school, but they had promised that they would try to get away later to help turn the flatboat. Although short for his age, Franklin was strong, and Allie was tall and sturdy-built, as George's father called it. They'd be a big help when it came time to pull the boat over.

The boatyard was humming with activity when George got there. He stopped where he was for a second when he saw Jefferson playing in the brown grass with another dog. He had intended to take time to hunt down his rambunctious little dog and tie him up in the shed at home. But he'd forgotten in his rush to get to the boat-turning, and he certainly didn't want to do it now. He might miss something. Surely Jefferson would stay out of the way.

His mind made up, George went down to the water's edge where his father and the workmen had already moved the heavy planked bottom of the flatboat from the construction area to the water by rolling it on large, smooth logs. Now that the bottom of the boat had been pegged together and sealed with oakum and pitch, it was time to flip the big wooden rectangle over into the water. Then the workmen would build up the sides and roof over part of the deck. After that the flatboat would be ready to float off down the Ohio River with a load of goods bound for Louisville or maybe New Orleans.

Every time George watched a boat-turning, he thought about how he and his family had floated down the Ohio on a flatboat just three years ago. Every week, lots of people arrived in Cincinnati, only to restock their supplies and keep traveling farther west to make a new life. He was glad that his family had settled in Cincinnati, even after that welcoming flood.

"Hi, Son," Father yelled to George.

George turned toward his father's voice. Father was arranging ropes and poles. Everything had to be done at the right time to get a flatboat turned.

"Did you bring your friends?" Father asked.

"They'll be here soon, I expect." George ran over to carry some more of the long poles that they would use.

"Charles, too?" Father asked. "We can use all the help we can get."

George frowned. "I didn't get to ask him. He was already gone." George didn't add that he had delayed getting out the door at school so Charles would be more likely to be out of sight. His conscience twinged a bit. He was coming

37

powerfully close to telling a lie to his father, and George did try to be honest. That was one part of the Bible that he understood for sure and tried to abide by. Now Charles was causing him to be dishonest to Father.

George hadn't really talked to his new neighbor since the *New Orleans* had left Cincinnati. Now that he thought about it, he hadn't seen Charles much since that ill-fated tour of the steamboat when the Jackson twins had teased the new boy about his scars. George felt a twinge of guilt as he remembered how he'd failed to defend his neighbor. Since then, Charles hadn't been around much other than at school. And even there, Charles had seemed to disappear at recess and during the break for the noon meal. Maybe Charles was doing the hiding now. The thought didn't make George feel any less guilty.

Shaking his head, George ran to help move the rocks that would be used for weights. He let thoughts of Charles fade. He had better things to think about like how to make it easier to turn flatboats. Getting these cumbersome boats turned right side up was a lot of work, and sometimes there were accidents that could lay a man up for months or longer.

There had to be an easier and safer way, and George had been working on that problem for some time now. He didn't have an answer yet, but he was determined to think of something. But for now he'd just watch and help do it the hard way. Maybe if he studied the process often enough, he'd figure out a solution.

The men had slid the boat partway into the water and were weighting one side of it with the heavy rocks. Once that side was securely weighed down, they would raise the other edge with poles until the flatboat was almost standing on edge. Then if everything went just right, they would push one side of the top edge with the poles and pull from the other side with ropes. Then the movement of the Ohio River's current would help flip the boat over.

That last pull was the tricky part. Strong arms and backs had to lean into the poles and pull on the ropes at just the right time. If the timing was off, someone might get seriously hurt. Generally the youngest of the men were the ones who took the poles since they had to be quick and agile to get out of the way when the flatboat started to turn.

George hoped he might get to work a pole this time. It had always been the ropes for him up until now, since they could be pulled in relative safety from well up on the bank.

"George, we're here," Franklin hollered down at him. George looked up the bank and saw his friend with Allie standing beside him. The two boys hurried down to help pile the rocks on the side of the boat.

"I was afraid we were going to miss it," said Franklin, as he struggled with a large chunk of rock.

"I had to get some wood in before I could leave," Allie said as he took the big rock from Franklin and heaved it onto the pile.

"Wood, wood. Always more wood," Franklin said. "Why don't you invent something, George, to take care of that chore? There has to be an easier way to heat a house and cook food."

George leaned over to pick up more rock before answering. "I'll think on that, but don't get your hopes up. Do you know for how many hundreds of years people have been heating their homes with firewood? You'd think someone like Sir Isaac Newton could have solved that problem instead of sitting under trees and getting hit by apples."

At last the side of the flatboat that was closest to the current of the river was weighed down to Father's satisfaction. It was totally submerged in the shallow water and showed no signs of being able to float up. The time to start raising the boat on the poles had come.

Father directed George and his friends to join the men who were attaching ropes to the other side of the boat. They would then pull the ropes taut while standing on the bank and adjust the rope lengths to keep a steady pressure on the ropes as the other men used poles to lift the edge of the boat.

George ran to obey his father, although he still wished that he could help with the poles. Allie and Franklin also took up ropes. One of the men double-checked the knots to make sure they wouldn't slip. At a command, the men on the ropes began to pull.

"Let's get some poles set!" George's father yelled. Other workers rushed to lift the far edge barely out of the water. Quickly poles were wedged underneath the lifted edge to hold the boat's weight. "Give us more pressure on the ropes."

George dug his feet into the riverbank and pulled harder. The pole-setters pushed longer poles in under the far side. Several times they repeated the process of pulling the ropes and pushing in longer poles. Just when George was sure they would never succeed, the big rectangle of boat deck was lifted high. The river rushed around the sides of the near edge, which was still firmly weighted down by rocks.

George had positioned his rope in back of his shoulder so that he could lean back into it and be able to pull with more of his body weight. Suddenly he found himself flying backward toward the ground. When he landed, the force of his fall knocked the breath out of him. Looking at his hands, he realized what had happened. His rope had snapped about a foot above his grip. From his position on the ground, George could look up and see the top of the boat waver a bit but then steady as the others took his share of the weight. His snapped rope was worthless.

George jumped up and looked around for something else he could do, but the rest of the ropes were already being pulled by the other workers.

Before George could decide what to do next, a small brown figure hurtled past him. Jefferson! The dog darted between the men and boys who were pulling the ropes. He stopped to sniff one and then the other and then began barking. He jumped up on Allie's leg and tried to lick his arm.

"Get down, you mutt," Allie ordered. "I'm busy." Allie was leaning back, pulling his rope just like the others.

"Jefferson! Come here, now!" George shouted. He didn't want to think of what would happen if one of the workers tripped over his dog.

George's words had no effect. The dog either didn't hear him or ignored his owner's stern command. So George took off after the furry troublemaker, who was now jumping up on Franklin.

Jefferson evidently saw his owner closing in and decided

this was some new game, for he raced past George and zigzagged on the bank until he was on the other side of the airborne flatboat deck. George was sure the dog would veer off and go back up the riverbank, because some of the other workers were wading in the water to set the poles and Jefferson had been leery of water ever since he had almost been swept away by the floodwaters when the Lankfords first arrived in Cincinnati.

But Jefferson was quick to see that there was a small sandbar jutting out into the Ohio. The workmen had taken advantage of that when they'd rolled the flatboat down to the water. At least some of the poles could be set from the sandbar instead of the water. Before George could grab him, the dog had run out onto the sandbar and begun jumping around Father's feet, barking enthusiastically.

"George," Father roared. "Get this dog!" George's father was trying to set one of the longest poles. The workmen were almost ready to try to tip the boat over.

"Yes, sir. I'm trying." George grabbed for the dog and missed. By now the workers were hollering at Jefferson, as well, and the dog was in a frenzy of excitement.

Suddenly one of the poles slipped. George saw the boat dip and one of the workers lose his footing as he struggled with his pole. George didn't hesitate. He splashed through the water and grabbed the pole that had slipped. He struggled to set it back in place. He heard his father yelling but could only strain to wedge the pole in place. It kept slipping in the soft river bottom.

Then other hands joined his, and together, George and the

other worker were able to jam the pole into the ground. The boat steadied, and George breathed again. Just then the current of the Ohio River took over, and the boat began to turn. George abandoned his pole and jumped through the water to flop on the sandbar. Once Franklin and Allie and the others who were working the ropes gave an extra tug, it took only seconds for the flatboat to topple over. The flatboat, ready now to be finished, bobbed gently on the Ohio River. Hopefully the success of the boat-turning would temper his father's anger at Jefferson's activities.

George felt movement beside him and remembered the hands that had helped him get the pole set. He turned to thank his helper and looked into the smiling face of Charles. George just gulped and smiled back. What else could he do?

CHAPTER FIVE

The Strange Migration

At last it was Saturday, and George finally had a few hours to himself. Chores done at home and at the boatyard, he headed for the old shed in back of the Lankford home. The boat-turning was still on his mind. His father had said that they were fortunate George's troublesome dog hadn't caused the flatboat to fall back and hurt someone, but he hadn't felt it necessary to punish George. He did make some pointed comments about showing responsibility for one's dog before being allowed the responsibility of handling a pole during a boat-turning.

Even Mother hadn't made too much of a fuss when she heard about Jefferson's antics. All in all, George felt pretty lucky. Or he would have if anyone other than Charles had jumped in to help him with the loose pole. There didn't seem any way to avoid that boy.

Shrugging his shoulders, George decided not to think about his problems. He was free to do as he pleased for an entire afternoon, and he planned to work on an idea that had been simmering in his brain ever since the *New Orleans* had steamed on down the Ohio River. He settled himself on a stool in front of a big wooden crate that he used as a desk in the shed. He liked to think of the shed as his workshop or even a laboratory.

George pulled his coat up around his neck. The late October days had finally acquired the usual nip in the air. That was the biggest problem with his workshop. There was no fireplace or woodstove, so it got downright chilly in the winter. But winter was still a ways off, and he had some inventing to do. He could ignore a little discomfort.

George had been asking questions this week. Questions about steam engines and steamboats. First he'd asked his father and Betsy's father what they knew about steam engines, and then he'd found out that a man who worked at the boatyard had just recently come from Pittsburgh. While there, the man had worked in the very boatyard where the

New Orleans had been built. He hadn't worked on the engine itself, but he had listened to the talk and watched the machinists as they worked to hook up the engine. He had been able to answer some of the questions George had wanted to ask Mr. Roosevelt.

George had thought about everyone's answers during every free moment he'd had that week. Now he was ready to begin. He picked up a piece of charcoal and poised his hand over a piece of brown paper his mother had given him. Sketches were always a good first step for an inventor.

George had decided to build a steam engine. Oh, it wouldn't be a big one of course, and he might have to make some changes if he couldn't get the right materials, but he was going to build some kind of steam-driven device. Perhaps he would put the device in a boat. It would be a small boat the size of a rowboat or even smaller, but the steam would make the boat move. His hand moved quickly over the paper as he sketched what he had learned about boilers, cylinders, and condensers.

He paused in his sketching for a moment. Surely this idea would interest the Jackson twins. They were always bragging about building secret projects. It stood to reason that they'd be interested in George's engine. Maybe he could work his way into their laboratory by getting them involved in this project. They could become the first boys in Cincinnati to build a steam engine. But before he approached Ted and Freddie about his idea, he had to have something to show them, so he went back to his sketching.

"George! You out here?" a voice called from up near the

back door of George's house.

George froze. He'd know that voice anywhere. It was Charles. What was he doing here? George felt like crawling under the crate and hiding. Couldn't he ever get away from that boy?

"George?" The voice was closer.

George quickly rolled up his sketches. It was no use. He couldn't hide; the shed was too small. There was no back way out, so he couldn't disappear. Better to get rid of Charles in short order so he could get back to his sketching.

"I'm coming," George yelled. He jumped off his stool and went to the door of the shed. "Hi, Charles."

Charles strode up with a wave. "Hi, George. Your mother said you were back here somewhere. What are you up to?"

"Oh, nothing much." George stepped out into the yard and pulled the shed door shut after him. He wasn't ready to tell anyone about his ideas yet, not that Charles would be interested. Besides, he didn't want to encourage Charles to hang around with him anyway, and if he started sharing his ideas with Charles, the other boy might get the wrong impression.

"Say, George, you want to come with me? I'll show you something really strange." Charles's scarred red face was lit up with excitement.

"What do you mean?" George wasn't the least inclined to leave his sketching at the moment, but he was curious about what could possibly have made Charles so excited.

"Just come with me, and I'll show you," Charles invited.

"I'm pretty busy," George said, running his fingers through his blond hair.

"You said you weren't doing anything," Charles argued. "Come on. It won't take long."

"Well, I was getting ready to do something," George replied. Yet another lie was catching up with him. And it was Charles's doing this time, too. He hesitated. "Oh, all right, but I don't have all day. Where is this strange thing?"

"Follow me," Charles answered mysteriously. With that, he turned and started for the street in front of George's house. George had to hurry to catch up.

The two boys walked at a good clip down the dirt road toward the edge of town, which was only a few blocks away.

"So where are we going?" George asked.

"You'll see," Charles replied and kept on walking.

George rolled his eyes. Why wouldn't Charles tell him what they were doing? If he weren't so curious about what Charles was going to show him, he'd turn around and head right back to his workshop. But how could he turn away from a mystery?

At last they started down a trail that led through the woods that bordered Cincinnati on the west side. George was getting more and more puzzled and impatient. He knew this trail, and it certainly didn't lead to anything exciting. But no matter what he said or did, he couldn't get Charles to tell him what was going on. Valuable time that George could use on his invention was being wasted. His frustration grew.

Finally he stopped. Hands on hips he demanded, "I'm not going another step until you tell me where we're going."

Charles put his finger to his lips, "Shhh. Listen." He stood still on the trail.

George shrugged and did as he was told. After a few seconds of getting used to the quiet, he became aware of a chattering, chirping kind of noise that grew steadily louder as he listened. He frowned and looked around. What was that sound? He'd never heard anything like it, and he couldn't see anything out of the ordinary. He raised his eyebrows at Charles in a silent question.

Charles motioned for him to follow as he turned off the trail and climbed through the brush up to a small bluff that overlooked a part of the woods that had fewer trees. Charles knelt down behind a big rock and waved at George to join him, then he peeked over the rock at something below.

George followed Charles and knelt beside him. He looked over the rock. At first he didn't see anything unusual, although the chattering sound was even louder. Then he saw movement. Movement everywhere. The trees and the grass under them seemed in motion. What in the world?

He pulled himself up over the rock a bit to get a better look. Then he realized what he was seeing. Squirrels! Dozens of squirrels. Maybe hundreds of squirrels. They were scampering across the grass and through the underbrush. They were climbing in the trees, leaping from one branch to another, moving as fast as they could. And they were all headed south. The noise he had heard was the chattering of all these small animals as they hurried on their way.

George and Charles sat and watched for a half hour while the squirrels passed. There seemed to be no end to the strange migration. Finally the line began to thin, and they could see the squirrels off in the distance starting to head toward the southwest. Even from that distance, the chattering of the squirrels could still be heard.

"What on earth is going on?" George finally asked Charles. "Squirrels don't go south for the winter. Are they running away from something or what?"

Charles stood up and stretched his legs. "I don't know. A trapper came into our store this morning and said that every squirrel in Ohio seemed to be on the move south. I didn't really believe him because he was saying lots of wild stuff. But I figured this was one tale of his I could check on, so I came out here to see for myself. This is what I found."

"It's a strange thing." George took one more peek over the rock, but the squirrels were finally out of sight. "Kind of spooks a body, in fact. I've never seen anything like it, and there's no telling where they're headed or why they're moving. I wonder what happens when they get to the river?"

Charles lifted his eyebrows. "Either they turn, or they jump into the Ohio."

"Not something I'd want to see." George made a face.

Charles nodded. The boys climbed down off the bluff and started back toward town.

"What other kind of wild stuff was the trapper saying?" George asked.

"He said that the squirrels running was a sign of bad things to come. That God was sending a judgment for all the evil that goes on."

George shivered. He wished his coat was heavier since the sun was dipping below the treetops, leaving the trail in shadows. "What else did he say?"

"That the floods in the spring and all the sickness after that were signs, too. Oh, and the comet. He really went on about that." Charles turned to George. "He said that the comet was a bad sign."

George nodded and kept on walking. There had been a comet trailing across the night sky for weeks now. It looked like a bright star with a long tail of sparkly smaller stars. His father said that comets didn't appear often, but that they were a natural occurrence. Still, it was an unusual event, and many people were reading some hidden meaning into it.

"Do you think the trapper's right?" George asked. "That the comet and the squirrels and everything else are a sign of God's coming judgment?"

Charles put his hands in his coat pockets. "Well, I don't know for certain, but it sounds kind of nutty to me. Didn't God send Jesus to die on the cross so that we could avoid His judgment?"

"That's what I was thinking," George replied. "I know God could punish us through disasters if He wanted to, but it doesn't seem like that's how He usually works. Not that I understand all that stuff."

"Yeah," Charles said. "I know what you mean, but my mother says that we aren't supposed to understand everything about God." The boys had reached the road that led back to town.

"That's what my mother says, too," George said. "I hope she's right." He looked at Charles and grinned. "But she usually is."

The boys walked in comfortable silence the rest of the

way into Cincinnati.

"Let's go down to the riverfront," Charles said when they reached their own street.

George hesitated. He really should get back to his sketches, but the afternoon was almost over and he wouldn't be able to get much done anyway. Maybe he could draw some tomorrow after church services. "Sounds fine by me," he said.

The boys headed for the river.

"I just remembered something else that trapper told us," Charles added. "He said that the Indians are scared stiff of the *New Orleans*. They call it a fire canoe."

"I guess I can see why," George said. "It sure did spit sparks, although canoe doesn't seem to be quite the right word."

Charles laughed. "Maybe they don't have a word for a bigger boat."

"I imagine you're right," George said. The boys walked east along the riverfront for a ways. "I suppose seeing something like the *New Orleans* would be scary if you didn't know what it was. The noise itself is pretty unsettling."

Charles nodded. They sat down on some crates and watched the wide Ohio River as it rolled past. There were a few flatboats coming into the docks to tie up for the night, but it was a pretty peaceful Saturday afternoon.

"Why do you think the *New Orleans* puts out so many sparks? I wondered if it was on fire when I first saw it," George admitted.

"My pa says that steamboats don't burn fuel cleanly, and lots of times they have to use wood that's too green or soft.

That makes lots of sparks and smoke and ash," Charles said. He absently rubbed the red scars on the side of his face as he stared out at the river.

"Do those hurt?" George asked and then immediately wished he could take the question back.

"What?" Charles turned to George. "Oh, you mean my scars."

George nodded. He knew he was being blunt, but some things just needed to be said. He hoped.

"No, not really." Charles didn't seem bothered by the personal question. "Sometimes they feel kind of tight. Especially when it's cold out. My mother has this special salve that I use, and it helps. Mostly I don't notice them."

George sighed. It was a shame that everybody else couldn't help but notice Charles's scars. There wasn't a spot on Charles's face that wasn't disfigured. He wondered if it was possible not to see those ugly puckered red scars every time he looked at the boy. George didn't think that was too likely.

"Look! Over there!" Charles interrupted George's thoughts with a shout. "Looks like a keelboat's coming in."

The shadows were starting to stretch out across the water, but George could see the boat slowly coming up the Ohio from the west. Even in the fading light, the man standing on the deck of the keelboat and directing all the activity looked familiar. A few minutes passed, and George, watching the boat approach, walked slowly toward the dock, trying to place the man on the boat. Suddenly he knew the answer.

"Why, that's Henry Shreve." George waved broadly.

"Captain Shreve!" he shouted. He was rewarded when the man returned his wave and shout.

"Captain Shreve is a friend of my family," George explained to Charles. "He comes to visit us when he stops in Cincinnati. He knows tons of interesting things and doesn't mind answering all my questions. He may have more information about these steamboats. Come on! You'll like him."

Charles's face was split with a big grin, and just for a moment George didn't notice the scars. Just for a moment.

CHAPTER SIX
The Accident

George and Charles waited on the dock while Captain Shreve and his crew brought the keelboat about. The crewmen set their poles in the river's bottom and slowly walked the length of the boat, pushing the boat forward. It was hard work and slow going against the current.

The boys knew that it took months for a keelboat to make

its way back up the Mississippi and Ohio Rivers after delivering a load to New Orleans. Every mile was hard won as they fought against the strong river currents.

"I think those fellows would like to have a steam engine for that boat," George said.

"I expect so," Charles agreed. "But then they wouldn't be able to hear each other."

George laughed. Keelboatmen were always loud, yelling insults from boat to boat or singing to help them keep poling in rhythm. A steam engine would surely drown out even their noisy progress up the river.

At last the keelboat was positioned against the dock and securely tied up, and Captain Shreve jumped off.

"Howdy, George," he called. "How's the family?"

"Just fine, sir. And yours?"

"Ah, George, I'm about to become a papa." Captain Shreve joined the boys. "I'm hurrying to get home before the big event, but my men need a rest, so we're spending the night here. We'll shove off tomorrow after Sunday services."

"Come and stay with us," George said. "My parents will be glad to see you again. We can take you over there now."

"Well, thank you for your kind offer. I certainly will at least go with you for a visit." Captain Shreve turned to Charles. "And who's your friend here?"

"This is Charles Lidell. He's our new neighbor from New York State. His parents have opened a new mercantile near our house."

Charles shook hands with Captain Shreve. "It's a pleasure, sir."

"Mine, too, son," the captain replied. "So, did you boys see the steamboat?"

"Did we ever," George said. "Did you see it, too?"

"Indeed. Got a good look at it in fact." Captain Shreve turned when one of his crew called out to him. He walked toward the man, who was still on the keelboat. "It was tied up at Louisville," he called back over his shoulder, "waiting for the water to rise."

"Do they have low water at Louisville?" Charles asked George as the boys watched the captain nimbly hop back on the boat to retrieve something.

"It's the falls," explained George. "I guess it's not exactly a waterfall, either, but that's what they call it. It's a stretch of rapids. Boats that sit deep in the water or are wide can't make it except when the water level is high on the river. The rocks get in the way, and either the boats get stuck or they get badly damaged."

"The *New Orleans* sits pretty deep." Charles frowned in concentration. "And the steam engine couldn't do anything about that."

George nodded in agreement.

"Hey, George." A voice interrupted George's thoughts about the draft of the steamboat. He whirled around to see the Jackson twins sauntering up the dock. He wanted to groan. Why did they always show up at the wrong time?

"So George, what are you up to?" Ted asked. To George's great relief, the Jacksons were ignoring Charles for the moment. "No signs of any other steamboats, I suspect?"

"No," George said. He wasn't sure how to handle the twins

when Charles was around, but Charles himself seemed unconcerned. He didn't appear to even be listening to the other boys. His attention was on the keelboat and the bustling activity that surrounded it.

"We've got some steamy news ourselves. Right, Ted?" Freddie asked his brother as he laughed at his own joke.

"We sure do," said Ted. "The steamiest." The brothers laughed loudly.

George sighed. Sometimes it was hard to remember just what it was that he liked about these two. Then he'd remember their laboratory. "What are you talking about?"

"Oh, just a steam engine that may be coming to town," Freddie said.

"A steam engine? How's that?" They had George's complete attention now.

Freddie raised his eyebrows. "Oh, we really can't say. At least not in present company." He looked pointedly at Charles. "Let's just say that it's a venture our father is developing."

"Your father is getting a steam engine?" George asked. "Do you mean a steamboat?" This was exciting news if it was true. He'd give anything to get a closer look at a real steam engine.

"As I said, we really can't talk about it here." Freddie gestured slightly with his head at Charles, who had turned away from the keelboat and was rejoining the other boys.

"You can come back to our house, George, if you want," Ted said. "We could talk about it there."

George wanted to shout yes and take off down the street after Ted and Freddie. He could see their famous laboratory and find out what all this talk was about steamboats. But he didn't shout yes. In fact he thought about going over and kicking a nearby post. It was so frustrating. He couldn't just up and leave Charles standing there, and he knew there'd be a big scene if the other boy tried to come along. Why did the long-sought opportunity to see the Jacksons' laboratory have to arrive at such a bad time?

"I can't go," George said abruptly. "I've got to take Captain Shreve back to my house. You'll have to tell me later."

Freddie shrugged. "Maybe we will, maybe we won't." With that the two brothers strolled off down the street behind the dock.

"You could have gone," Charles said quietly.

"No, I couldn't," George snapped. "So just forget it."

"Ready, boys?" Captain Shreve joined them once again. "Sorry for the delay."

"No problem, Captain," George said. "Let's get on home though. We might be in time to order up something special for supper. In honor of your visit."

"Good thinking. Although I've yet to eat anything your mother cooked that wasn't special," the captain said.

That night at the Lankford house turned into a party of sorts. After a big supper that gained lavish praise from Captain Shreve, the Lankfords were joined by Betsy and her parents and Charles and his parents.

Betsy played her violin, and there was lots of talking and a few tall tales. The favorite topic was the *New Orleans*. George and Charles sat on the floor near Captain Shreve so they wouldn't miss a word.

"I'm telling you, Paul," Captain Shreve said to George's father, "the high-pressure steam engine for a steamboat is going to be common in a few years."

"Henry, those contraptions are dangerous." George's father handed the captain a cup of coffee. "Why not stick with the low-pressure engine like the *New Orleans* has? Mr. Roosevelt seems to think it works well."

"Not enough power." Captain Shreve sipped his coffee. "Oh, the low-pressure engine will pull the load some of the time. But not unless the conditions are just right."

"Is that why the *New Orleans* is stuck at Louisville?" George asked.

"No, lad, not really. But that brings up another problem I was mentioning to Mr. Roosevelt just the other day." Captain Shreve chuckled. "He wasn't particularly pleased to hear it, either."

"What did you tell him?" George had a hundred questions he wanted to ask.

"That the draft of that boat is just too deep. It sits so low in the water that the hull will be scraping every sandbar between Louisville and New Orleans. No, that hull needs to be a lot shallower."

"But where would the machinery go?" Charles asked. It was the first time all evening that he had spoken up.

"That, my friend Charles, is the question everyone is asking." Captain Shreve waved his tin cup in the air. "And I don't yet have the answer. But I will, I will. It's only a matter of time."

The mantel clock chimed ten o'clock before everyone reluctantly left for home. It had been a grand evening, and as George lay in bed, he felt as if his head would spin right off with so many questions and new thoughts. He was more determined than ever to build something that was propelled by steam power. The sooner he could get to work on it the better.

It turned out to be several days before George could do anything with his invention other than think about it. He decided finally to undertake some experiments with steam before building his steam device. Captain Shreve and George's father had explained how a steam engine worked, but George wanted to see for himself. So on Thursday after school, he began setting up an experiment.

It was cold and a little windy, but he was tired of waiting. He built a small fire as close to the shed as he dared, trying to block the cold wind. His mother's old washtub would be the boiler. He filled it with water from the well and placed it on a makeshift stand over the fire. While he waited for the water to boil, he rigged together what he hoped would work as a condensing chamber.

Betsy's father, Dr. Miller, had given him a large green glass bottle with a narrow neck. This George attempted to suspend upside down over the water with a harness made of string. Captain Shreve had explained about the vacuum that condensing steam made.

If the experiment worked right, the steam would rise into the glass bottle. Then George would lower the bottle just a little, so the neck of the bottle was in the water. Next he would put out the fire and wait for the steam in the bottle to cool and condense. When it did that, the water should rise through the neck of the bottle to fill the vacuum created by the condensing steam. Easy enough if everything worked.

The first step went just fine. It took awhile, but at last the water got hot. George used a couple forked willow sticks to get the bottle apparatus balanced over the washtub before the water started to boil. The problem would be lowering the bottle enough so that the water could be sucked up after the steam condensed. The string harness kept the bottle upside down, but the steam was going to make it difficult to lower the bottle. He needed some big gloves to protect his hands.

George studied the contraption for a moment. Maybe the neck of the bottle could be placed in the water to begin with. Would steam still collect in the bottle? He wasn't sure, but it was worth a try. Besides, experimenting was all about trying things to see if they would work.

He lowered the bottle into the water. Steam was starting to rise, and it was hot. George moved as close to the fire as he dared. Was steam rising into the bottle? He thought it was, but as the water began to boil hard and clouds of steam rose into the cold air, his view of the interior of the bottle became clouded. It was just about impossible to tell if there was any steam in the bottle. Was it time to put out the fire? If he couldn't be sure that there was steam in the bottle, he certainly couldn't tell if there was enough steam in the bottle yet.

A blast of cold wind came roaring around the corner of the shed. The cloud of steam shifted, and George attempted to hop out of the way. His foot hit one of the blocks holding the washtub off the fire. Before he could shove the block back with his boot, the washtub began tipping over.

Without thinking about the heat of the steam, George grabbed for the sticks holding up the bottle. He just wanted to keep his bottle from breaking. He yelped as the steam hit his hand. Immediately, he jumped back, tripped over the block, and fell on his back. The washtub plopped upright into the middle of the fire, shooting out sparks in every direction. Wind lifted the sparks, and in seconds the brown grass nearby was dotted with tiny fires.

George's hand was throbbing, but he struggled to his feet. He had to get those fires out. They could burn down the shed, or even the Lankford's house. All too often, people lost their homes to fire, and George didn't want to be responsible for making his entire family homeless. Images of some of his friends' burned-out homes spurred him on. Ignoring the pain in his hand, he desperately fought the tiny flames. How would he ever be able to get all these little fires out in time?

Suddenly he felt someone stomping the ground behind him and turned to see Charles grinding out each tiny fire with his heavy boots. Seeing that one problem was being attended to, George looked around and noticed that the shed was getting scorched by the heat of the main fire. He hurried to use his extra bucket of water to put out that fire, still blazing around the washtub.

Finally they were done. The fires were out, and steam sizzled up from the area where the water had hit the hot flames. George sat down on the ground, exhausted.

"Are you hurt?" Charles asked as he leaned over George.

"Not much," George replied, squeezing his eyes shut in an attempt to keep the tears from falling down his face. His hand felt like someone had mashed it in a vise, but he didn't want to admit that to Charles. "My hand's a little burned."

"Let me see," Charles demanded.

"It's fine." George picked himself up off the ground and attempted to casually dust himself off, but he couldn't hide the grimace that twisted his face when his burned hand rubbed against his clothes.

Charles gently pulled the injured hand out to look at it. "This is a nasty burn," he said, his voice full of sympathy.

George looked directly into the other boy's brown eyes. "How bad?" His voice wasn't steady.

"Oh, not this bad," Charles said as he pointed to his own hand. "But it needs to be looked at. Come on. I'll go with you to Dr. Miller's."

"Do I have to go there?" George surveyed the ruins of his experiment and the blackened grass and shed. He'd be hearing more about this, and if Betsy's father treated his hand, George wouldn't be able to downplay his injury.

"You could have your mother look at it," Charles suggested with a grin.

"On second thought, I guess seeing Dr. Miller would be just fine," George said. The last thing he needed right now was for his mother to get all upset over this little accident.

CHAPTER SEVEN
Scientific Setbacks

"George, what on earth?" It was Betsy who opened the door to her father's surgery. Since she had finished her schooling, she often helped her father with his practice. "What happened? Come on in."

She guided George over to a chair. Charles followed along and stood nearby.

"I just burned my hand a little." It was all George could do to keep from crying or jumping up and down. He wasn't sure which would help the pain more, and he'd never felt pain like this before.

"Let me see," Betsy ordered. Gently she took his arm and pushed back the cuff of his coat sleeve. She held his injured hand up to the light coming in from the window and carefully examined her cousin's burn. "This really hurts, doesn't it?"she said in a surprisingly gentle voice.

George allowed himself only a grunt in reply. He was busy taking deep breaths to fight the pain, and he was afraid that if he said anything, he'd start screaming. The situation was bad enough without embarrassing himself in front of Betsy and Charles.

"A burn is always painful," Betsy said, "but this one could be a lot worse. I don't see any blisters yet, and that's a good sign."

"Can you do anything to make it stop hurting so much?"

Betsy nodded. "We can try at least. Charles, would you please take that bucket to the pump and fill it with water?"

Charles jumped to do as Betsy asked.

"So let me guess, George," Betsy said as she opened up the medicine cabinet and looked over the bottles and jars in there. "This is the result of one of your experiments gone wrong."

"Well, sort of," George said. "I was trying to condense steam in a bottle your father gave me, but then the washtub slipped. I grabbed for the bottle because I didn't want it to break, and one thing kind of led to another. When it was all over, I was left with this." He held up the offending hand.

"Seems like God was looking after you today," Betsy said

as Charles hurried in with the bucket of water.

George frowned. Why did people always say that? If God had truly been looking out for him, He would have kept that steam from burning George's hand.

"Charles, please put the bucket here on this stool," Betsy directed, pointing to a stool she'd placed in front of George's feet.

Charles rushed to comply.

"Here, George, stick your hand in this bucket of water," she said after the bucket was positioned.

"Why? My mother always puts lard on a burn." George pulled his hand back. After all Betsy was just his cousin, not a doctor.

"That's one remedy, but my father says if a burn doesn't have blisters yet, it's better to put the injured area in cold water. It will help the pain. Later we'll put some salve on it."

That decided George, and he leaned forward so that he could plunge his hand into the water. It was achingly cold, but instantly the throbbing pain ceased.

"It worked," George said in surprise.

"If you're all right, George," said Charles, "I've got to get home and do my chores. I'll stop by your house and make sure that fire is out."

"Thanks. I'm fine." George sighed as he watched Charles go out through the surgery's front door and head up the street toward the Lankford's house. He knew he should be grateful to his neighbor for turning up to help, but it just made everything that much harder.

Betsy was looking at him quizzically. There was no need

to get her going on the subject of Charles. He had a sneaking suspicion that he knew what she'd say, and he didn't want to hear it.

"Will this still blister?" he asked and lifted his hand out of the water.

"Maybe not," Betsy answered. "As I said, you're fortunate."

"What you said before about God looking after me, I mean." The pain in his hand was quickly returning, so George quickly shoved it back into the cold water. "I don't understand that. If He was really looking after me, wouldn't He have stopped the steam from burning me at all?"

"Sometimes I wonder about that, too," Betsy admitted, brushing back some stray curls from her forehead. "Especially since I've been helping my father with the doctoring. He says that God doesn't always rescue us from our mistakes. Sometimes He doesn't even rescue us when it's not our fault. It's one of the mysteries of God." Betsy leaned on the examining table.

"Like with Charles," George said and lifted his hand out of the water again. "He was just a child. He didn't know any better than to pull that kettle over on himself."

"True, but from what Charles's mother told mine, he should have died from his burns. So maybe God did rescue him."

George thought about that for a moment. Charles didn't seem bitter about his scars. Maybe he was just glad to be alive.

The surgery door flung open.

"What have we here?" Dr. Miller came into the room in a rush of cold air, shedding his hat and jacket as he entered.

"Oh, it's nothing," George assured him, but he knew that if he had ever had any wild hopes that his parents would somehow not notice the results of his failed experiment, they were dead now. Between Betsy and her father, to say nothing of Charles stopping by to make sure the fire was out, there was no way his parents wouldn't learn about George's misadventures. Something told George that his experimenting was about to be curtailed.

Two days later George sat dejectedly on the riverbank watching the Ohio flow by. Another Saturday, but as he'd feared, he was forbidden to work on his steam experiments. He looked at his bandaged hand. Only two small blisters had raised after his accident. But that didn't matter to his mother. She had said enough was enough. He was to leave the steam to Mr. Roosevelt.

In a last effort to save his project, George had appealed to his father. But Father had simply glanced toward the scorched shed and commented that they were lucky the house was still standing. George, Father declared, needed to have some time to think about the importance of safety when he was experimenting. George hadn't argued the case any further. He knew a hopeless situation when he saw one.

George laid back in the brown grass and stared at the blue sky above. The weather had turned warm again. Quite warm for November in fact. It was a perfect day to work on his invention. But his father had been quite clear on the subject of fires: George couldn't use fire in his experiments until he heard otherwise. George had to admit that the scorched shed and blackened spots in the grass hadn't helped his case.

He rolled over and lay on his side, watching a flatboat drift by. Parents just didn't understand the scientific process. An accident was simply a small setback, something to learn from or it would be if he hadn't been forbidden to work with steam again.

"See anything worth seeing?"

George looked up to see Charles standing over him. Charles was following George's gaze out toward the river. George took a moment to really study the red scarred face above him. It didn't seem quite as startling as it had at first. Maybe he was just getting used to it. Too bad the other kids at school didn't feel the same way. The Jackson brothers had been taunting Charles just yesterday.

"No, not really," George replied. "The same old flatboats and a keelboat or two." He sat up, and Charles sat down beside him.

"Is your hand better?"

"It's fine. Almost." George plucked at the grass sticking up in front of him.

"Can't do your steam experiments anymore?" Charles continued to stare at the Ohio.

"Nah," George answered. "How'd you know?"

"Betsy."

The pair sat in silence for a few minutes. George resisted looking around to see if anyone was watching him sit with Charles. It was kind of nice to sit there with the other boy.

"Why not work on something else?" Charles asked.

"You mean another experiment?" George flipped some

grass over his shoulder.

"Sure. Something without steam."

"But that's what I'm interested in," George protested. "I want to build a steamboat or at least some kind of steam-driven device."

"Maybe you can get to that eventually," Charles said, his brown eyes twinkling. "After the grass grows back and your hand heals and the shed collapses so your parents forget about the scorching."

George gave Charles a rueful grin. "After the smoke clears, you mean."

Charles grinned, too. "Exactly. Meanwhile, work on some other part of the project."

"Hmm." George frowned in concentration. "I see what you're saying. I can't work on the steam engine part of my model steamboat, but I could work on the design of the other parts."

"Right." Charles leaned back on his arms. "Something like the hull design."

"Hull design." George dropped a handful of grass and turned to Charles. "Captain Shreve was talking about that the other night. Also about where to place the paddle wheels and the machinery." He jumped up and walked back and forth on the bank. "I could work on those things and power the boat some other way. And maybe if I figured out how to have a model steamboat sit higher in the water, the principles could be carried over to the larger boats."

Charles nodded and brushed his trousers off as he stood up.

"But how?" George stopped his pacing. He stood staring

out at the Ohio for a few moments. "Maybe some kind of paddle boat. With something to push the paddles."

"I've heard of paddle boats powered by horses or oxen," Charles said. "Full-sized boats."

"You don't say." George considered this idea. "Guess that would be too big for me to build."

"It would take a fair-sized boat to use a horse to power it," Charles agreed. "But there must be some other way to use the idea."

"Maybe a one-man paddle boat?" George resumed his pacing. "It could use good old foot power."

"Sounds like it would work," Charles said.

"We can do it," George said eagerly. "It will take some work, but we could be paddling down the creek in no time. It'll be great."

He paused. That's when he noticed the odd look on Charles's face. He understood the look, too. In his excitement, George had included Charles in his plans. And why not? In an instant George decided his course. "You will help me, won't you?" he asked.

Charles hesitated and looked directly into George's blue eyes. "If you really want me to," he said. At George's nod, Charles smiled and thrust out his hand to shake on the deal with his new partner.

A distant clanking noise distracted George. He jerked around to stare down the Ohio. "What's that noise?"

"I don't know," Charles said, "but it sounds like. . ."

"The *New Orleans*!" George finished. "It's coming back! It's coming back upstream."

"It really is coming against the current," Charles said. "Mr. Roosevelt and Captain Shreve were right."

"Of course they were." George started scrambling down the bank toward the dock. "Come on. Let's get a good place to watch." The two boys started running, and George could see that a lot of other people had also heard the noisy engine. It was louder than ever, and he supposed that the added noise was because the engine was laboring against the power of the river's current. But the engine was winning the battle.

The dock quickly filled as the shops near the waterfront emptied their Saturday crowds when word spread that the *New Orleans* had indeed returned. The crowd was loud. Everyone voiced his or her opinion on this latest event. Most vowed that the boat coming upstream was only what they had expected. A few suspected some kind of trick, although they couldn't explain exactly what that might be.

George and Charles found some stacked wooden crates of merchandise to climb up on. This gave them a narrow perch that offered a good view of the incoming steamboat.

"Look," George yelled. "There's Mr. Roosevelt and his wife. And the dog, Tiger." He shaded his eyes against the afternoon sun. "Mrs. Roosevelt is holding a baby, I think. I guess she had her baby since they were here."

"I wonder why they came back," Charles said. "You don't think they've given up on going down the Mississippi do you?"

"Of course not." George gave Charles a disgusted look. "They would never do that."

"You're right," Charles agreed. "Maybe they just want to prove to people that a steamboat can go against the current."

"They've sure done that," George said with satisfaction. This day that had started out so gloomily was finishing up just fine.

"Hey, George!" A familiar voice lifted over the din of the crowd.

George looked down to see Freddie Jackson standing on the dock below the crates. His brother Ted was right behind him.

"Let us up there with you so we can see," Freddie hollered.

George shrugged. "Sure, come on up." He scooted over and bumped into Charles.

"There's not enough room for all of us, George," Ted said. He grinned, but George didn't find it to be a very friendly smile.

"We'll make room," George offered and moved over as far as he could.

"I'll get down," Charles said.

"You don't have to do that," George protested. But before he could continue, Charles had leaped down off the crates and moved some distance down the dock. George could only watch the other boy go. He wanted to holler and tell Charles to come back or even jump down and follow him, but he didn't.

Ted and Freddie jumped up beside him. "Thanks, George. You're a pal."

George just nodded. Pal wasn't the word he'd use to describe himself after the way he'd just treated Charles. Why had life turned so complicated since Charles had arrived? And now he had asked Charles to help him with the boat. What would the Jackson brothers say when they learned about that decision? One more problem to deal with.

Bad News

For once George was glad to be wrong. Working together on the boat with Charles didn't turn out to be the problem he had feared it would be. Without even talking about it, the boys established a pattern. At school they ignored each other, but after school and Saturday mornings found them scurrying to get their chores done so they could meet in George's shed and work on "the invention," as they sometimes called it. So far, the Jackson brothers didn't seem to be aware that George and Charles were working together on anything.

George thought of the two of them as partners in a venture

rather than as friends. When he allowed himself to think about the circumstances at school, it was plain to him that Charles was the one who was keeping to himself. George obviously wasn't ignoring Charles. Charles wasn't around to be ignored. What they were doing in their free time was strictly business.

Some days Charles and George labored over the design for their boat, and other days they spent searching for materials at the boatyard and the mercantile. George's father let him have free choice of the scrap wood, and he even threw in a few pieces that weren't scrap. Charles's father was a saver, so a search of the storeroom at the mercantile yielded many odds and ends that the boys could use to good advantage.

"What length did we finally decide on?" Charles asked. He was stacking the wood scraps just outside the shed door. It was a fine Saturday afternoon in the middle of November, and the boys were clearing the shed out so they could build their boat inside.

"I don't think we decided, exactly," George replied as he pushed some storage boxes to the side of the small space they were clearing. "At this point I guess the biggest factor is that it has to fit in this area right here." He held out his hands to indicate the cleared space. "And it's going to be cold in here when we have to leave the door open."

Charles shrugged. "Got to have the light from the door. That lantern your mother loaned us helps, but it's still dark in here without any windows."

"That's for sure." George shook his head as he looked around the small shed. It was better than working in the yard, but not much. At least they wouldn't have to worry about getting

76

snowed on or the boat getting wet. He couldn't help comparing his rickety shed with the laboratory that the Jackson brothers supposedly had in their big barn. He knew for a fact that the barn outside their fancy house even had a few glass windows. Maybe those windows opened into their laboratory. They'd have plenty of room and light for their experiments and as the weather grew colder, Ted and Freddie would be able to stay plenty warm.

George had barely seen the Jackson twins during the last couple weeks. They often disappeared somewhere during recess at school and hurried home when school let out. Neither boy had mentioned their father's steam engine again. George figured they were working on a big project themselves. Well, he'd have something to show them before long.

"We forgot to bring those old kegs from the back of the store," Charles said, interrupting George's thoughts. "Let's finish cleaning up here and go after them. My ma might have some apple tarts left in the pantry. I could handle one of them. How about you?"

"Oh, I could probably manage," George replied with a grin. "All this work helps build up a fair-sized appetite." He began working faster to clean out the corner of the shed.

A half hour later George and Charles had forgotten about the kegs, but they were enjoying apple tarts at the kitchen table at Charles's house. The house was only a few steps from the back door of the Lidells' store. Charles had told George that in New York they had lived upstairs from their store, so a separate house was quite a luxury to his family.

At last the tart-stuffed Charles and George remembered their errand and hurried out back to locate the kegs. Mission accomplished, they each grabbed a keg and started around to the front of the store.

"George. Charles." It was Betsy calling. She hurried down the sidewalk with a basket over her arm, long cloak flapping, curly brown hair peeking out from under her hood. Emily was walking twice as fast to keep step with her taller friend.

"What are you two up to?" Emily asked. She was practically puffing, she was so out of breath.

"What's your rush?" George countered with his own question.

Emily looked at Betsy and giggled. Betsy frowned. "No rush." As she spoke, her eyes shifted to the door of the mercantile behind George. "So what did you say you two were doing?"

"I didn't say," George informed her, "but nothing much is what we're up to."

"You're never up to nothing much, George," Emily said.

"That's right," Betsy agreed. She pointed to the kegs the boys were carrying. "Anything dangerous here?"

"Not yet," Charles answered, "but maybe soon."

Betsy started to speak but stopped abruptly. George saw her face turn faintly pink. Again she was staring at something in the store before she dropped her gaze. George frowned. What in the world was wrong with his cousin? Just then he heard the sound of the front door of the mercantile opening and shutting.

"Betsy, er, Miss Miller. It's good to see you again."

George whipped his head around and almost groaned aloud. It was Andrew Farley, and he had that moony look on his face again. George had come to like Andrew a lot, but the young man turned positively silly when Betsy appeared. Which seemed to happen all the time lately.

"It's nice to see you, Andrew," Betsy said. "I was just going to pick up some items from the store." She smiled sweetly and dropped her gaze again.

"Have you heard the news?" Andrew asked.

Betsy shook her head and glanced at Emily, who shrugged slightly. "No. I don't think so."

"What news?" George stepped up to ask.

"There was a big Indian attack up in Indiana Territory." Andrew turned to include George and Charles. "On the Tippecanoe River."

"Settlers?" Betsy asked with a stricken look on her face.

"No, army infantry and some Indiana militia."

"What were they doing up there?" Charles asked. "That's way up north in the Territory. The Tippecanoe feeds into the Wabash."

"I guess some of Tecumseh's bunch were making some threatening noises. There's a band of Indians living up there at a place called Prophets Town." Andrew took Betsy's basket from her. "Let me carry this for you."

"I heard last week that Tecumseh was trying to stir up a bunch of different tribes," Charles said. "He wants them to join together. I guess he's a real influential leader among his people."

"My father says the British are making trouble, trying to stir up the Indians," Emily said.

"He's right," Andrew said. "The talk is that they're prodding the Indians to fight us."

Betsy's face was pale now. "What will happen? Were there a lot of soldiers and Indians killed?" she asked softly.

"Enough," Andrew answered and put his hand on her elbow. "But the Indians were chased out and then Prophets Town was burned to the ground. So it may all be over."

"Or it may be just the beginning," Charles said. His usual smile was missing.

"We have to pray about this," Betsy said firmly.

The others just nodded.

Distracted by thoughts of Indian attacks or even war with England, George didn't hear anyone approach until a hand was clapped on his shoulder. He jumped in surprise and jerked around to see Ted Jackson standing beside him. Freddie was nowhere in sight.

"Howdy, George. What's up?" Ted swung an empty cloth sack in a circle with one hand, making the others in the group keep at a distance.

"Did you hear about the Indian attack?"

"Sure did. My father had word of that yesterday." Ted gave his bag a swing. "Guess we showed those dirty red Indians. They won't come messing around here anymore."

"They were there first," George burst out. "They had a settlement, and it got burned to the ground."

Ted made a face. "So? This is America now. Those Indians will just have to move somewhere else." Ted paused and then gave an exaggerated imitation of someone who'd suddenly remembered something. "But of course, I nearly forgot. You're a red man lover."

He jabbed his finger in Charles's direction and smirked. "Maybe you ought to join your people," he called to Charles. Ted turned his back and started toward the store. "I've got to get on," he called over his shoulder. "Got to pick up a few things for a little project Freddie and I are working on."

George stood there for a moment and stared after Ted. Suddenly his arm was grabbed, and he was whirled around. His eyes came to rest on Betsy's face. It was pink again but not from embarrassment. She was angry. She pushed him back down the sidewalk a few steps.

"Why did you let that weasel say something like that about Charles?" Her eyes were sparking with fury as she put her finger in the middle of George's chest. "Well?"

George didn't say anything. He knew Betsy was right, but it just seemed like the right words didn't come out at the right time. Something about the Jackson twins made him freeze up.

"The Bible has a lot to say about loving your neighbor as yourself, George Lankford." Betsy backed off a few inches. "I suggest you remember that sometime soon."

Back held stiffly straight, she marched back to where Andrew stood talking to Emily and Charles. She held out her arm to Andrew, who jumped to take it and lead her into the store.

"Come on," Charles said as he walked toward George. "Let's get these kegs back to the shed. We've still got time to get started."

George took one of the kegs and followed Charles without a word. He was thankful that Charles didn't seem to expect him to talk about what had just happened. He didn't know what he could possibly say that could explain his behavior.

The next morning during church services, George tried harder than usual to listen to the preacher's sermon. He tried to listen every week, but usually his thoughts skittered away to one of his projects. His thoughts this Sunday morning were of Indian attacks and war and Charles. These topics weren't nearly as pleasant to dwell on as his usual daydreams, so he made a determined attempt to fill his mind with the preacher's words.

Betsy had barely glanced his way before the service when she slid into the pew in front of him. Surely she wasn't still angry about yesterday. She looked tired, as if she hadn't slept well that night. He dismissed the idea that she was still angry. Betsy got mad at him frequently, but she forgave quickly, too. Maybe something else was wrong. He sighed softly as they all stood for the final prayer. Life had seemed a lot easier a few short weeks ago.

The Millers and the Lankfords filed out of church together and gathered in a little group on the sidewalk outside to talk. George pulled his coat closer. The November wind was biting, and the sun's weak rays peeking through the gray clouds did nothing to provide any warmth.

"We've had news from Boston," Betsy's mother stated. George didn't understand the grave look on Mrs. Miller's face.

"Letters?" George's mother asked.

Betsy's mother nodded. "We received them late last night. It was too late to bring them to you to share."

"Is it bad?" George's father asked.

"Not good," Mrs. Miller answered, "but on the other hand," she straightened her shoulders and lifted her head, "not the worst, either."

"Richard is still missing," Dr. Miller said. "Benjamin and

Martha have exhausted their last diplomatic channel for getting him returned by the British. Many missing boys have been returned, but the British claim that Richard can't be found. They say that he's dead."

"He's not dead," Betsy said fiercely. "I would feel it. We were friends. He's not dead." Her words trailed off, and George saw that her green eyes brimmed with tears. Betsy had always had a special bond with her cousin. Her violin had been Richard's. He had given it to her to keep before he went to sea.

"No, we pray not, Betsy," George's father agreed. "In fact, that's just what we need to do right now—pray."

Dr. Miller nodded and stretched out his hands. The others quickly formed a circle right there on the sidewalk.

Dr. Miller prayed in his deep voice: "Lord, we ask that You would keep Richard as close to Your heart as he is to ours. Protect him and bring him home safely to his family." Dr. Miller paused. "We also ask that You would bring an end to this talk of war. That You would enable all peoples to live together peacefully and that justice would reign. We thank You for the blessings You have provided in such abundance to us. In Jesus' name we pray. Amen."

George murmured his own "amen." He looked over at Betsy to see if she was feeling better and saw that Andrew had slipped up beside her. The young man stood quietly holding Betsy's hand, a concerned look on his face. For once George didn't feel like groaning.

CHAPTER NINE
The Big Shake

The weeks passed quickly. For once, George didn't see much of the Jackson brothers. He and Charles spent all their spare time hammering and sawing in the shed. Their craft was taking shape despite a few setbacks. Building a boat, even a small one, was certainly not as easy as George's father made it look. He told the boys that sometimes the bigger size of the boats he worked on actually made the task easier than what they had undertaken.

One cold day in the middle of December, George stood shivering in the shed, staring at the boat. Charles was helping at the store and would be along as soon as he could. They were finished with the construction of the boat itself. Now it was time to build the paddle wheel and rudder.

"George, you in there?" a voice called from up by the house.

George shoved his dog, Jefferson, who was standing in the door, out of the way and poked his head out to see that it was Franklin and Allie.

"Sure," he yelled. "Come on in." He hadn't seen much of his friends lately, what with being so busy with boat building and all.

The three boys spent the next few minutes examining the boat. Franklin and Allie had lots of opinions to offer on its seaworthiness.

"It's so flat," Allie said. "It looks like a raft with sides and a prow."

"It's almost as big as a skiff," Franklin said, "but it doesn't have a keel. Why did you decide on such a strange shape?"

"There are a couple of reasons for that," George answered. "We're trying out a flat hull design because Henry Shreve said that's what steamboats will go to eventually. He says they'll be flat with the paddles in the back."

"Why?" Allie asked.

"It will let them go on much shallower water."

"What's the other reason?" Allie asked as he circled the craft.

George shrugged and grinned. "We couldn't lay a keel if

our lives depended on it."

The others laughed.

"Say, did you hear about the Jackson twins?" Franklin asked as the group moved out of the crowded shed.

"They weren't at school today, but that's not so unusual. They seem to disappear for days at a time," George replied. "What's up?"

"Their father has packed them off to Pittsburgh to visit relatives," Allie answered as he leaned over to rub Jefferson's ears. The small dog had plopped himself on Allie's feet and was looking up at the boy with pleading eyes.

"So what's so odd about that?" George raised his eyebrows. The twins were always coming and going to Pittsburgh or Louisville or cities even farther away.

"It's the reason for their being sent away," Franklin explained. "They almost blew up their barn."

"Blew up the barn!" George exclaimed. "How in the world did they manage to do that?"

"It was just a small explosion actually," Allie said. "Franklin and I were with his father at the mill when Mr. Jackson was telling about it. He said the boys had managed to blow out some of the glass windows when they were trying to build some kind of cannon. They were using chemicals without his permission."

"He said that he was sick of them running wild when he had to work such long hours," Franklin added. "So he was sending them to stay with their grandfather for a while in Pittsburgh."

"They don't like staying there," Allie said. "I've heard

them talk about it before. Their grandfather is real strict."

"Yeah," George said, "I've heard Ted say that it was like jail there." He wasn't sure how Ted would know anything about life in jail.

"I'm glad they're gone," Allie said. "They're mean. Even if they are kind of funny sometimes."

"They're mean all right," said Franklin, "but my ma says that they don't get much attention from either of their parents. Maybe that makes them mean."

"Maybe," Allie said doubtfully. "But I still won't miss them. I guess they'll be getting plenty of attention from their grandfather in Pittsburgh, just not the kind they like."

George didn't say anything. Actually it was a relief for the twins to be gone. He could just concentrate on the boat and not worry about when they'd show up and what they might say to Charles next.

"What will keep that boat from leaking and sinking?" Franklin asked, changing the subject. "I saw some cracks between the boards."

"George's father is going to caulk it," a new voice answered.

The three boys turned and saw Charles walking up to where they were standing.

"Hi, Charles," said Allie. "Your boat is looking great."

"Thanks, but it's George's boat. It was his idea. I'm helping a little." Charles leaned over to pet Jefferson, who had moved over to stand by him.

"What's wrong with Jefferson, anyway?" Allie asked. "He's usually running around everywhere and hardly pays any attention to us. But this afternoon he keeps coming up and standing against first one of us, then the other, begging to be patted."

"I don't know," George replied and leaned over his pet with concern. "He's been acting kind of strange for a day or two, hanging around the shed door, trying to sneak into my bedroom at night. I've never seen him like this."

"Is he sick?" Franklin asked.

"I don't think so," George answered. "His nose isn't dry, and he's still eating. A dry nose is supposed to mean a dog is sick."

"My nose is dry. How about yours, Charles?" Franklin reached up to elaborately examine his nose.

"Nose check time." Charles also felt his nose. "I'm sorry to report that my nose is quite dry. However, I find that my appetite is entirely intact."

"Then we must only be partly sick," Allie said. He too made a show of examining his nose.

"I've had enough of this," George said. "I don't know what's wrong with the dog, and I sure don't know what ails you three, but I'm going home to supper." Tossing his head in disgust, he turned on his heel and headed toward the front door of his home.

The other boys grinned at each other and hurried after him.

That night George felt like he had hardly gone to sleep when he was awakened by Jefferson's howling. To protect Jefferson from the extreme cold, George's mother let the dog sleep in a corner of the kitchen in the wintertime, right below George's small bedroom. When Jefferson started howling from down in the kitchen, it sounded like he was right beside George's ear.

At first George covered his head with his pillow to block out the sound. It didn't work. The dog's howling was almost a wailing sound. It kept getting higher and louder. George sat up in bed. He had never heard Jefferson make such a noise before, and he knew that if he didn't do something about it soon, the rest of the family would wake up, too. Mother would not be pleased if Lucy's sleep was interrupted. A tired two-year-old had a way of making the whole family suffer.

Quickly he slid out of bed and pulled on his trousers. The floor was icy, so he stuffed his feet in his shoes as he stumbled down the stairs toward the kitchen.

"What's wrong, boy?" George said in a low voice as he entered the dark kitchen, which was lit only by the faintest glow from the banked fire in the fireplace. The dog's howling ceased. Instead he began to whimper.

George made his way over to the corner, sat down beside Jefferson, and pulled the small dog close.

"Are you sick?"

With quick and gentle hands George examined his pet. The dog's nose was still cold and damp, and Jefferson didn't flinch when George carefully felt his stomach and back.

"You seem fine."

George settled in next to the dog and leaned back against the wall. As his eyes grew more accustomed to the dark, he saw that Jefferson seemed focused on something in the middle of the room. No matter how hard he stared, George could see absolutely nothing out of order in the kitchen. The big clock ticked loudly on the mantel but that was the only sound, and there was no movement of any kind. What had so captured Jefferson's attention?

Briefly George considered whether or not there might be a thief in the house somewhere. But he remembered one time when Dr. Miller had come unexpectedly in the middle of the night to get George's father to help him with a patient. Jefferson had barked himself silly and growled and made all sorts of commotion, even after he realized that the intruder was a familiar person. The family had joked the next day about George's fine watchdog.

So it didn't seem likely that some prowler could be what was bothering Jefferson. George sat quietly beside his dog for a few moments, just listening. He couldn't hear anything, but suddenly the hair on the back of his neck began to prickle just a little. He strained to see in the darkness, but there just wasn't anything to see.

Jefferson began to whimper again. What was wrong!

A low rumble caused George to let out the breath he had been holding. He could relax. It was just a thunderstorm coming. That was odd in the middle of December, but not unheard of. But then the rumble didn't ebb like thunder did. It continued to grow louder. And come to think of it, Jefferson didn't usually get upset by thunderstorms.

Suddenly the floor under George seemed to dip and slide away. Jefferson yelped as the pair found themselves sprawled flat on the kitchen floor. The floor suddenly rocked in the opposite direction, and George and his dog were thrown back against the wall. George tried to grab something to hang onto, but everything in the room seemed to be moving. Terrified, he clutched at Jefferson and waited for whatever force this was to bring down the house around him. He was certain he was going to be killed. He could only pray that the rest of the family would somehow manage to escape in one piece.

It felt like a lifetime but was probably only a minute before he heard his father's voice yelling from the front hallway. "George, where are you?"

"I'm here! In the kitchen!" George screamed back.

"Come on, Son! We've got to get outside."

"I'm coming." George stood up and found that he could walk if he allowed himself to move with the rocking motion. He hurried as quickly as he could toward the hallway. The mantel clock crashed to the floor in front of him as he passed the fireplace. He skirted it, only to bang into a small chest that seemed to be working its way across the wooden floor.

At last he was in the hallway where Father was bundling Lucy and Mother into a blanket and out the front door.

"We've got to get outside, George. Come on."

"What's happening?" George grabbed the staircase railing to steady himself.

"It's an earthquake!"

"Earthquake!" George's jaw dropped. He'd heard of earthquakes, but he didn't know they could happen in Ohio.

"Out! Now, George," his father ordered.

George obeyed. But wait, where was Jefferson? He turned

91

back toward the kitchen.

"Jefferson," he yelled. "Come on, boy. Don't be afraid."

A streak of brown fur shot across the still rocking kitchen and out the front door. George was right behind him.

The Lankford family practically tumbled onto the brown grass in their front yard. George's mother had the blanket wrapped around herself and Lucy. She opened it and pulled George up next to her. George's father stood over them. Still the ground rocked back and forth. How long would this last?

George's mother pushed Lucy to a sitting position on the ground and pulled the blanket up around her head. George and his mother knelt over the young child to form a protective shield over her. George felt his father lean closer and wrap his arms around all of them.

George could hear more than he could see as he sat huddled there on the grass. It was night, anyway, so he wasn't sure how much he would have been able to see if he weren't bent over with his family. The loud rumbling had ceased, but now buildings throughout the neighborhood popped and cracked. Dogs barked, and people shouted as they, too, scrambled out of their homes into the inky darkness.

Behind the Lankfords, a loud rumble signaled that the brick chimney on their house had suddenly tumbled down. Chimney bricks landed within a few feet of the huddled family. George felt his mother flinch but then straighten.

"It's time to pray," she said. Her voice was calm and strong with only a tiny quaver to let George know that she, too, was terrified. "Lord, we ask only that You show us mercy in this awful upheaval. Please protect us and all the others feeling this great unleashing of nature's power. We are your servants. Amen."

A tiny bit of George's fear subsided as he sat there with his family while the earth continued its tormented rocking. God was still in charge. He began praying silently. He wasn't sure later how long he prayed.

It seemed like hours, but he knew it could only have been a few minutes before the earth ceased its swaying as suddenly as it had begun. For a moment, Cincinnati was covered with an eery silence. It was as if all of the town was waiting to see what would happen next.

"Is it over?" George finally asked his father, who had straightened up to look around. George was suddenly aware that Lucy was crying loudly beneath him. Rather than sounding frightened, she sounded angry at being so wrapped up and confined. He moved over slightly so that his mother could have more room to pick up the child.

"Perhaps only for the moment," George's father replied. "Or perhaps for good. I don't know much about earthquakes, but I've heard that there's often more than one tremor at a time."

"What do we do?" George stood up and pulled the blanket closer around his mother and Lucy's shoulders. He stepped over next to his father.

"We wait, son. That's all we can do." Father put his arm around George's shoulders. "We stay out in the open where it's safest and wait for dawn. And we pray."

George just nodded.

"However, I will dash into the house for some more

blankets and coats." Father rubbed George's shivering arms. "It's right nippy out here." He turned toward the house.

"Paul, don't go in there," George's mother ordered. "It may not be safe."

"I'll be careful, Ellie." He leaned over and touched her cheek. "You and Lucy need shoes and coats."

"I can help." George stepped forward.

"No," George's father said. "You stay here with your mother and Lucy. It'll only take a minute for me to go in and grab a few things."

"Yes, sir," he said and watched his father run into their house.

"Where's Jefferson?" George's mother asked as she adjusted the blanket around Lucy, who was trying to struggle free.

Evidently Jefferson heard his name because suddenly he was at George's feet, tail wagging so hard that his whole body was moving.

"I guess you're just fine, boy." George knelt down and hugged his dog, who seemed to have had a better sense of what was coming than his owner.

The dark streets quickly came to life. Lanterns made points of light as people ventured out to check on their neighbors. Voices called back and forth, echoing reassurances that people were all right, even if their homes weren't.

Father had just stepped out of the house with the extra blankets and clothes and George had finally started to relax a little when the earth trembled again. The tremor passed more quickly this time, but it was still unnerving.

Once the motion stopped, George's father settled Lucy and Mother on the grass in a nest of blankets. Soon Lucy was asleep again. George couldn't help envying his little sister. He didn't know if he would ever be able to sleep again.

Finally the sky began to lighten in the east. The long terrible night was almost over. Now they would be able to see how bad the damage was.

"I'm going to check on the Millers," Father announced, standing up.

"I'm going, too," George declared, springing to his feet.

"No," Father said. "I need you to be here with Mother and Lucy so that I don't have to worry about them, too. And if there's another tremor, your mother will need your help."

George reluctantly settled back on the blankets next to his mother. "Yes, sir," he said and watched glumly as his father headed down the street.

A few minutes later, George jumped at the sound of his name.

"George, is everyone all right?" It was Charles. He and his father came striding down the street in the early morning light.

George quickly stood up to greet the two. "We're fine. And you?"

"We're all in one piece, but the mercantile is a mess," Charles replied. "I don't think a single thing is left on the shelves."

"That's true," Mr. Lidell said, "but it isn't important. What's important is that we're all safe." He tipped his hat to George's mother. "If you're all in one piece, ma'am, I'll be going on down the road."

"Thank you, Mr. Lidell," George's mother said. "My husband has gone to check on the Millers."

"I'll stay here," Charles said. Mr. Lidell nodded and with a final wave went off down the street.

George plopped back down on the blanket and motioned for Charles to join him. "What have you seen so far? Is there much damage? What was it like at your house?" George's questions poured out.

He had wanted to go with his father to see if Betsy and her family were safe, but he also was just itching to see what had happened. It didn't seem quite so frightening now that the darkness had receded, and he wasn't planning on experiencing too many earthquakes in his life, so he wanted to learn everything he could from this one. Besides, he figured when he was an old man, people would want to hear about the great earthquake of 1811, and he wanted to be able to give lots of details.

The boys sat on the blanket and traded stories while George's mother talked to another neighbor who had joined them. Lucy woke up and crawled into George's lap, where she sat quietly sucking her thumb.

Then without warning the ground began to rock again. The daylight revealed an odd picture as the earth seemed to sway and dip in what almost looked like waves of water. George clutched Lucy to his chest. Once again the air was filled with cracking sounds and crashes and the occasional tinkle of breaking glass. This time it was over much more quickly, ending with a final violent plunge that threw George and Lucy against Charles. George heard a loud crash nearby before the quiet descended again.

It was only a few moments before there was movement and shouting in the streets. In minutes Father ran up, closely followed by Mr. Lidell. As soon as Charles's father saw that he was safe, he ran on past to check on Mrs. Lidell, who was staying with an elderly neighbor.

When things settled down again, George and Charles walked around the corner of the house to investigate the crash that they both thought had come from the backyard.

There they found a pile of boards where the shed had been. The old shed had already been there when the Lankfords had built their house three years ago, a remnant of a former landholder whose home had burned. George's father had often talked about rebuilding it but had never had the time. Now the poorly built structure had been scattered by the force of the earthquake.

"It's just gone!" George said and ran toward what was left of his workshop.

"The boat," Charles said. "What about the boat?"

George's heart plunged to his toes. The boat was under all that debris. He skidded to a stop. How could he not have thought of that first? All that work, all that effort, and now it wasn't even visible. Was there anything left?

CHAPTER TEN

Danger in the Schoolhouse

George's first impulse was to start tearing away at the boards that covered the area where the boat had been stored. But before he could act, the earth gave another minor tremor. He gulped and looked at Charles.

"As much as I want to find out what happened to the boat," he said, "we'd better get back to my mother. She has enough to worry about right now without wondering if we're safe."

Charles nodded in agreement and the two boys reluctantly returned to the growing group of neighbors who were talking with George's mother.

As the morning passed, the earth stopped trembling so often, and Father and Mr. Lidell decided to check out each other's houses and the mercantile together. Because they didn't want anyone else inside the buildings until they were sure the structures were safe, they gave George and Charles permission to sort through the rubble of the shed and discover what had happened to their boat.

The boys rushed to the backyard and anxiously started moving the flimsy boards aside.

"It's amazing the shed didn't collapse before now," Charles said, holding up a termite-infested board.

George looked ruefully at all the tunnels the insects had bored in the piece of wood he was holding. "Father always meant to build a new shed," he said, "but work at the boatyard had to come first and he didn't want me trying to do it by myself. Mother was worried that I'd hurt myself."

"After the success of your steam engine experiment," Charles teased, "who could blame her?"

"You had to remind me."

Just then, George caught a glimpse of newer wood. "Charles, look! The boat or what's left of her must be under here."

The boys poured all their energy into removing the last few boards from on top of the boat. When she was at last uncovered, the boys sighed together in relief.

"We'll need to repair the hull there," George said, pointing to a cracked board, "but other than that. . ."

The two boys examined every inch of their boat and could find no other damage.

"George," Mother called. "I need your help."

"I'll be right there," George yelled. He looked at Charles in frustration. "Just when we were getting somewhere."

Charles sighed. "Let's prop the boat up beside the house for now. It's time I got back to my house anyway. By now our fathers probably have plenty of work for us to do. Something tells me it may be a while before we can work on this boat again."

"We didn't know the half of what this cleanup would be like," George muttered to himself a few days later as he worked at cleaning up the debris that remained scattered in his backyard. There didn't seem to be an end to the fallen branches and broken glass and pottery. Just cleaning up the kitchen had taken the Lankfords the better part of two days. They were thankful the earthquake hadn't managed to scatter hot ashes from the fireplace onto the kitchen floor. Father was also busy getting the boatyard in working order again.

While he worked, George thought about his own boat-building project. The loss of the shed for a workshop was going to be a problem. The weather was turning much colder— too cold most days to do the more detailed work that remained. Not that anyone in Cincinnati had time for much of anything besides cleaning up.

George stacked the splintered pieces of wood. The last few days had not been easy for anyone. Although the damage wasn't deemed major by the few people in town who knew anything about earthquakes, a lot of brick chimneys had tumbled down, and a few of the older buildings had a collapsed wall here and there. Most of the damage was from anything and everything bouncing off shelves and tables and out of cupboards. And that had created quite a mess.

Betsy had described to George how the bottles of medicine at her father's surgery had crashed to the floor out of an unlatched cabinet. The Lidells' mercantile was a total wreck. Fortunately not much merchandise had been damaged, but it would be days before the mercantile would function smoothly again. George had helped both Betsy and Charles with the cleanup at their homes.

He stopped working for a moment as a now familiar tremor vibrated the ground he stood on. He sighed as it passed. His mother was right when she said that the worst loss from the earthquake was the loss of peace of mind, for the earth continued to shake at the most unexpected moments. Oh, it was a slight trembling. Most of the time it was barely perceptible, but it kept everyone on edge, wondering if each small tremor would suddenly worsen.

Stories had already been carried back about worse damage down the Ohio and Mississippi Rivers. Trappers and boatmen arrived at the Cincinnati docks with tales of falling river banks, disappearing islands, and worse.

The most fantastic story George had heard had come from an old trapper who said he had stood on the bank of the

Mississippi and watched it flow backward for a time. George tried over and over to picture the kind of upheaval that would make the mighty Mississippi River reverse course. He suspected that the trapper was exaggerating, but in any case, the grizzled old man was in his own words, "Hightailing it back East where the ground stayed put the way it was supposed to."

George straightened the stack of damaged wood one last time and started back to the warm kitchen. He wasn't so sure that the old trapper didn't have a good idea. He'd heard many stories about the generations of his family that had lived in Boston. They'd survived hurricanes, fires, and even the Revolutionary War, but they'd never had to live through an earthquake.

George couldn't help thinking about that other trapper who had told Charles about the squirrel migration back in October. Maybe the squirrels had somehow sensed the coming earthquake and decided to get to safety. It was a puzzle. But then Jefferson and the other dogs in the neighborhood had certainly known something was about to happen. Maybe animals were aware of changes in nature that people didn't notice. One thing was sure: no one had expected an earthquake to hit Ohio.

The next week brought Christmas, but it was a subdued celebration. George usually loved the holiday, but it was hard to concentrate on the traditional festivities when a body was wondering if the first shake was only the beginning of disaster. George's mother said that hard as it might be, they would still celebrate the birth of God's Son.

So they did, and George found that it was possible to live

with the small tremors that had become a daily event. He fell into the habit of silently praying a short prayer each time the trembling began. And since the tremors were happening so often, George was doing more praying than he had in a long time.

George had been taught to pray before he fell asleep when he was a tiny child, and he certainly tried to listen and pray at family devotions and in church, but this was different. His prayer during the tremors usually went something like this: "Thank You, God, for keeping us safe and please, please, continue to do so."

He wasn't entirely sure if that's how a person was supposed to approach prayer, but it seemed right. Besides, his mother had said on more than one occasion that God met us where we were. George had never really understood that phrase, but now he thought it just meant that God didn't require fancy prayers. That He would listen and help no matter how simple the prayer. So George prayed, and gradually life began to return to normal in spite of the tremors.

George was carrying wood into the kitchen one cold January day when Charles, with a huge smile on his face, came hurrying around the side of the house.

For just a second or two, George looked at Charles's scarred face and realized that he hadn't noticed the other boy's scars for days.

"Guess what?" Charles said, but proceeded without waiting for George to respond. "Our neighbor Mrs. Deering says that we can use her shed to finish the boat." Charles grabbed some wood from the pile and caught up with George. "Actually it's better than a shed. She called it a summer kitchen. It's hooked onto the back of her house."

"That's great," George said. "But what will she use for a kitchen? She sure won't want to be cooking anything while we're shaping wood and creating piles of sawdust."

"My mother says that Mrs. Deering is from the South, where sometimes they have a summer kitchen. It's just used in the summer when they want to keep the heat from the fires out of the main house. The rest of the year they use a normal kitchen like we do." Charles shrugged. "I don't think summer kitchens are used much around here, but Mrs. Deering likes to have things the way they were when she was young."

"So this summer kitchen has a fireplace?" George dumped his wood in the woodbox in the kitchen. The possibilities began to dance through his head.

"Sure does, and we can use it. Mrs. Deering said that she might be old-fashioned about some things, but she'd never want to stand in the way of science."

"How'd she find out about the boat?"

"I told her," Charles replied. "I hope that was all right," he added hesitantly. He dropped his load of wood into the woodbox, too. "She was interested in what we were doing before the earthquake that kept us both so busy. I didn't think you'd mind."

"Oh, no. I don't mind. I'm just surprised that she would want to help us." George imagined how some of their other neighbors would have been likely to respond to a similar request. Not that he could blame them. Through the years his

104

projects and inventions had sometimes spilled over into the neighbors' property. Seldom with good results, he had to admit. And Jefferson had not always been careful about where he dug for bones.

"I think she misses her grandsons," Charles said. "They went to live in St. Louis last spring. She may join them this year."

"Well, what are we waiting for?" George pushed the kitchen door open again. "Let's get the boat and tools moved over there." It was past time to get back to work on the invention. The cleanup was over, and now they could do work on the boat in spite of the cold weather that was gradually icing up the Ohio.

The minor repairs that the boat hull needed were quickly accomplished in the relative comfort of Mrs. Deering's summer kitchen. Mrs. Deering herself was a source of some delicious cookies that she brought, hot from her other kitchen, out to the boys. She'd occasionally ask questions about their work, but she didn't hover—an attribute that George appreciated. Soon the boat was ready to be hauled to the boatyard for caulking.

George consulted with his father about the caulking one night at supper, and Father agreed that the boys could take the boat to the yard that Saturday. He would caulk the boat during odd moments at the yard and let them know when it was ready. In the meantime, the boys would work on the paddles and rudders.

George thought Saturday would never come, but finally school was over for the week, and he and Charles made plans for the weekend. As soon as they were finished with their Saturday chores, George and Charles met in the summer kitchen, picked up the boat, and headed out toward the boat-yard.

After they had delivered the boat, they stopped to stare at the Ohio. It was almost totally iced over after the frigid days and even colder nights of the past few weeks. George shivered and pulled his heavy coat closer. It might only be the end of January, but it seemed a million years had passed since he had stood and watched the *New Orleans* steam its way toward Louisville for a second time. Having proven to the skeptics that his steamboat could go against the current, Captain Roosevelt had left Cincinnati, promising that his third visit to the city would come only after a successful trip down the Mississippi. George wondered if Captain Roosevelt and his family had made it safely to New Orleans.

He knew that they had finally made it past the falls at Louisville, because the story of their trip through the rapids had been repeated many times. It had been touch and go whether or not the *New Orleans* could make it through the shallow rapids. But at last they had been successful.

Now had the earthquake stopped them? Where had they been when the Mississippi ran backward, if that tale was true? Surely someone would come up the river after the spring thaw with some news. Right now there were only questions, and there was no way of finding out the answers.

The paddle wheel assembly for the boat went together smoothly in Mrs. Deering's summer kitchen, but the rudder was another story. George and Charles had several spirited discussions about how to steer the craft.

At last they decided to use two small rudders for more control. The pilot would have a rudder stick for each hand while he turned the crank with his feet. The crank would drive two belts, one on either side of the boat, which in turn would drive the paddle wheel mounted at the back of the boat on a wooden framework.

Would it work? George wasn't sure, but he intended to see.

"This is looking good," George said one afternoon after school. He was putting the finishing touches on the paddle wheel.

"If you do say so yourself," Charles said with a laugh. He looked up from where he was using a small knife to carefully shape one of the rudders to get just the right curve.

"Well, I do." George jumped up to put another chunk of wood in the summer kitchen fireplace. "How soon do you think we can test this?"

"You mean put it in the water?

"How else?" George rubbed his hands in front of the fire. It was so cold that the fire didn't really warm the drafty room.

Charles paused. "We've got to get this all assembled, and we've got to do something about getting belts for the crank. And then there's a slight problem with the water."

George frowned. "What problem?"

"It's not water right now. It's ice," Charles said. "Pretty hard to launch a boat like this in ice."

"Oh, yeah," George said with a sheepish grin. "Ice. Forgot about that little detail." He sighed. "Guess there isn't much to be done about that. Or at least I haven't thought of anything yet."

"The thaw will come eventually, and we just might have this thing put together by then." Charles held the rudder up. "I think this will do." He carefully placed it on an old table that they had moved into the summer kitchen. "I've got to get home and do my chores."

"Me, too," George said and started picking up his tools. "Say, have you looked at the pendulums today? Seems to me like they're vibrating more."

Charles joined George in front of an old chest that sat in the corner of the summer kitchen. George had rigged a series of pendulums there. They were small pieces of hardwood of different lengths suspended from a framework by string. He had spent hours making sure they were exactly level, but the effort had been well worth it. Whenever the earth shook, the pendulums swayed. Of course the stronger tremors could be easily felt, but the pendulums showed that there were dozens of slight tremors that a person couldn't perceive.

"I noticed that earlier." Charles joined George in front of the pendulums. "Do you think it means anything? That they're moving more, I mean."

George watched the pendulums sway gently. "I'm not sure. Probably not." He had fixed these pendulums after visiting with a friend of his father's. Dr. Drake was keeping records of the earth's shaking and had explained to George how pendulums let people know of tremors that they wouldn't otherwise notice. George had decided to try it himself. That had been several weeks ago, and it seemed like his pendulums were moving more every day.

"Shaky ground or not, what are we going to do about belts for the crank?" Charles asked as the boys continued cleaning up. "We really need leather for them."

"I'm thinking on that," George answered. "Just haven't had any real inspiration yet. But between the two of us, it'll come. We've made it this far, and I'm not about to let a shortage of leather keep us from success."

George woke up early the next morning when Jefferson jumped on his bed. He had been dreaming about belts and pendulums and rudders.

"What are you doing up here, boy? You'll get skinned alive if Mother finds you." George shoved at the dog. "Get on down."

Jefferson refused to budge. Finally George gave up and crawled out of bed and got dressed. It was earlier than he usually got up, but the sun was rising and it was obvious he wasn't going to get any more sleep if Jefferson had anything to say about it. The small dog followed him downstairs without protest.

George spent his extra time before school thinking about the problem of getting leather to make the belts. They might be able to use something else, but what? The belts on the machinery on the *New Orleans* had all been made of leather. He could get scraps of leather, but that wouldn't be enough material. The belts would have to be several feet long.

George was still working this problem around in his mind when he got to the schoolyard. He was so lost in his thoughts that he stumbled over a rock.

"What's wrong, George?" Allie asked as he walked across the schoolyard toward his friend. Franklin was right behind.

"Nothing's wrong, Allie," Franklin said and gave George a pat on the back. "George here is just getting old. Can't see where he's going and probably can't hear much either."

George laughed. "Actually you must be right. I think my brain is shrinking or something." He told his friends about the problem with the belts. "I just can't seem to come up with a solution."

Franklin frowned in concentration as the three of them headed for the school door. "I know what we can do!" he suddenly exclaimed. "I'll ask my father. You know they use belts at the mill where he works. Maybe there'll be some old ones they can't use anymore."

"That's a terrific idea," George said. "I hadn't even thought about that." He clapped his friend on the back. "Good thinking, Franklin."

"So what are you thinking up, Franklin?" a different voice piped up from just inside the school doorway.

"It was something to do with the mill, I do believe," added another voice.

"Well we should know about that, shouldn't we?"

George spun around. The Jackson brothers! Evidently they were back from Pittsburgh, and it didn't sound as if their trip had reformed their rude habits any. George sighed. It had been so quiet the last few weeks. He had almost forgotten the

Jacksons and their tricks. Almost.

Just then, Charles came charging up the steps. He stopped short when he saw Freddie and Ted, but he didn't say a word. He just grinned and went on into the school.

"What's he got to smile about?" Ted asked. The bell began to ring, and they all moved inside.

"I'm sure I don't know," Freddie answered his brother. "He's just as much a freak as he was before we left."

"Now, wait a minute," George spoke up. "Just leave him alone. He can't help how he looks."

"George, George," said Ted, "aren't you the hero?"

George opened his mouth to respond but something stopped him. Suddenly there was a roaring sound in the air. Like thunder, but not thunder. In the tenth of a second before the ground leaped under him, he knew what was going to happen. It wasn't going to be the usual small tremors. This time they were in for another big shake.

Children screamed around him. Crashing furniture only added to the chaos. The floor seemed to rise up to meet George, and he found himself thrown against the wall with Allie on top of him. The strong shakes continued as the boys tried to get up.

"Get out. We've got to get out," Charles shouted over the noise.

George finally heaved himself up to see that Charles had two younger children by their arms and was attempting to herd several others toward the door.

"Take them out," George shouted back to his friend. "I'll get more."

In seconds George had pulled another group of small children out to the schoolyard, where they all piled into a heap. The teacher shoved a few stragglers out the door and came out himself. The ground continued to rock, but they were much safer now that they were out in the open and away from flying books and crashing windowpanes.

In a few minutes the earth stood still. It was quiet except for the whimpering of the younger children. George pulled himself up. The buildings were still standing, and everyone seemed to be in one piece.

Then he saw the Jackson boys. They sat apart, clutching one another. Pale-faced and big-eyed, they stared ahead in what looked like terror. George spared only a moment's thought to them before turning his attention to the children who needed comforting. It appeared that Freddie and Ted weren't quite as brave as they liked to think they were.

CHAPTER ELEVEN
Surprise!

It was cleanup time again. George thought it went much faster this time than after the first earthquake. Maybe it was just that most people had carefully repaired latches, secured large pieces of furniture, and devised other ways to lessen the damage a quake could cause.

Or maybe they felt like he did. He was ready to get on

with life. The earth might continue to shake and tremble, but he wasn't going to sit around and wait for some final catastrophe. He was going to trust God and enjoy life.

George had reached that conclusion after a long day and night of anxiety, thinking about the second quake and wondering if a third would come. At last he decided that there was nothing he could do to keep an earthquake from coming, so he needed to simply trust God.

It was hard at first to let go of the worry, but his mother often said that God was faithful. George wished that her words meant that God would prevent the earthquakes from coming, but if that couldn't happen, then he would trust that God would always be there to help no matter what.

So work resumed on the boat. The hull had escaped damage this time since it was still at the boatyard and George's father had developed better ways of securing and protecting the boats he was working on in case of another earthquake. George and Charles made fast progress assembling the crank, and then one afternoon Franklin showed up at the summer kitchen with a huge smile on his face.

"Look. I got it." He held out a large, awkward bundle.

George dropped his tools and reached for the bundle. "What did you get?"

"You got the leather for the belts, didn't you?" Charles said. He put down the crank parts he was working on.

"Sure did," Franklin replied. "My father got two old ones at the mill. They have worn spots and can't be fixed to use there."

"But we can cut out the weak spots and sew them back

together since we don't need this much length," George said as he examined the long strips of leather. "Good job, Franklin." He slapped his friend on the back.

"It was nothing," Franklin said, but his grin got bigger, if that were possible.

"This is terrific, Franklin," Charles said, adding his thanks. "Now we just have to figure out how to sew them up."

"Hmm," George said. He wrinkled his forehead and twisted his fingers though his straight blond hair. "It's too heavy to sew with a regular needle and thread, isn't it?"

"Afraid so," Charles answered. "That leather would just rip through ordinary thread even if you could get a needle through it, which you couldn't. And I don't think any of our mothers would be willing to donate one of their fine sewing needles to the cause." The three were quiet for a moment as they thought over this problem.

George snapped his fingers. "I've got it. Andrew was talking a while back about repairing harness for their oxen. He must have the tools to sew up leather. We could ask him if he'd help us."

"Good idea," said Charles, "but would he have time? I heard that there was a lot of damage to his father's barn and sheds from this last quake."

"Betsy did say something about that yesterday." George shrugged. "So we offer to help with the cleanup. Then maybe he'd have the time in a day or two to help us fix our belts."

"Sounds fine," Charles said, and Franklin nodded in agreement.

"Besides," George added, "he's so sweet on Betsy, he'd

probably drop everything to try to impress her by helping us."
George was still trying to dislike Andrew Farley for the way
he acted toward Betsy, but it was getting harder. If he helped
them sew up the leather belts, it might become impossible.

That evening George saw Andrew and asked him about the
leather belts. Andrew was glad to help with the belt sewing.
He said it wasn't necessary for the boys to come help with
the repairs at the farm, but George said that it was only fair.
He spent several evenings after school helping Andrew with
all the extra earthquake-related chores. Charles came when
he could get away from the store, and Franklin and Allie
helped some, too.

"If nothing else," Andrew observed to George one
evening, "when all this is done you'll be quite a hand with a
hammer and saw. What between repairing these barns and
building that boat of yours, you're spending about as much
time on carpentry as you are on your schoolwork."

One Monday night at supper, Father had an announce-
ment. "Well, George, your boat will be ready for you on
Saturday."

"You mean Charles and I can go get it?" George asked,
finding it hard to believe that his father had managed to get
the caulking done with all the extra boat repairs the latest
earthquake had brought in to the yard.

"Yes," Father said, his eyes twinkling. "Can't have that
boat taking up valuable space, though we'd better not have
you pick it up until after you've done the chores your mother
has for you."

Yet again George watched another school week drag by. He decided that waiting was the hardest thing he had ever had to do. Saturday came at last. As soon as he and Charles were done with their chores, they raced to the boatyard, where they were going to meet Franklin and Allie. There was much to be done because the boat had to be hauled from the boatyard back to the summer kitchen, and then the work of getting everything assembled could begin.

Andrew was also going to meet them at the summer kitchen because he needed to get exact measurements for the length of the belts before he could sew them.

George and Charles stood for a few minutes on the bank of the Ohio while they waited for their friends. The other boys had promised to help carry the boat, which was a little heavier now that it had been sealed up. Besides, Franklin and Allie didn't want to miss out on the final assembling of their friend's craft. George noticed that the Ohio was still iced over across most of its width. It had been warmer the last few days, but not warm enough to cause the ice to break up.

"No boats coming down now," he said to Charles. "But it won't be long before we see some river traffic if the weather stays this warm."

"Doesn't seem possible that spring will be here soon," Charles said.

"The boat might be ready to launch in a couple weeks," George said. "I've got the rudders figured out, I think. If we should get a good warm spell, the creek and mill pond will thaw in a couple of days."

"Is that where you want to test it?" Charles asked.

"Seems like a good place. And you know our parents wouldn't let us take an untried craft out on the Ohio."

Charles nodded. "We've just got to get everything together first. I hope it doesn't sink."

"It won't," George said with conviction. "It's seaworthy."

"You mean creekworthy?" Charles asked with a laugh.

"Exactly. Hey, there's Allie and Franklin. Let's get moving on this job."

So the boat got moved and measured. The boys watched that afternoon as Andrew carefully cut and stitched the leather belts. He used a sharp kind of pick to make holes in the leather and then drew thick threads of rawhide through the holes to make a strong seam. It didn't look hard, but George had a feeling that it wasn't as easy as Andrew made it seem. The finished belts were strong and had flat, hard seams.

At last everything was ready to be put together, but the day was over. The moment of truth would have to wait until later the next week. Would the foot crank turn the paddle wheel when it was connected to the belts? Or would George and Charles have to go back to the drawing board?

After comparing their families' plans for the week, the two boys decided to find the answer to that question on Thursday afternoon. They would do a dry run of the crank and paddle wheel apparatus. The rudders weren't finished, but that wouldn't affect the working of the paddle wheel.

That Thursday, Charles and George rushed to their workshop after school. They carefully balanced the boat on several empty wooden crates in the middle of Mrs. Deering's summer kitchen and began putting things together.

By the time they had put the belts on and tightened some joints, Allie and Franklin had shown up. In a couple of minutes Emily and Betsy appeared at the door. Soon after that, Andrew arrived. The summer kitchen was practically overflowing as George prepared to climb into the boat and work the crank.

"Guess you told a few people we were testing today," Charles said under his breath to George.

"I guess I did," George said with a grin, "although I can't say as how I remember doing it."

It took a minute for Charles to adjust the belts and give George the start signal. George leaned back in the small wooden seat and began pushing the crank with his feet. It was clumsy, but slowly the belts began to turn. Everyone watched to see what would happen. The paddle wheel gave a jerk and began to turn also. Just the way it was supposed to.

The room erupted with cheers. In a minute George climbed out to let some of the others have a turn at cranking. The boat was a fine sight sitting there with her paddle wheel spinning in midair.

"Will she work in the water?" Charles asked George as they watched Allie take a turn cranking. "The water will create more resistance than air does. Do you think the paddles are strong enough?"

"Sure they are," George answered. "But if it'll make you feel better, we can double-check all the joints and pieces to make sure we don't have any cracks or loose connections."

"What have we here?" The door opened and a voice rose

above the noise in the small room. Everyone turned to see who had spoken.

George saw a young man in the doorway. Tall with dark hair and a muscular build, he looked familiar, but George wasn't sure who he was. Then Dr. Miller appeared in the door behind the stranger.

A gasp nearby made George turn. It was Betsy. Her face was so pale it made her freckles look scarlet. She stared at the stranger in shock.

"Richard?" Betsy barely said the word aloud. She took a step toward the door.

George whipped back around to look at the young man. Could it possibly be Betsy's cousin? Gone for so many years and presumed dead by the British? Was Richard now here in Cincinnati?

The question was soon answered when Betsy launched herself across the room to hug the newcomer, who laughed and swung her around as much as was possible in the crowded room.

After a moment's hesitation, everyone else plunged forward to pelt Richard with a dozen questions. They all knew the story of his disappearance and were interested to know how he had managed to escape from the British.

"Wait. Wait." Dr. Miller's voice boomed out. Behind him stood George's father and mother and Betsy's mother. "We'll be having a celebration tonight, and you and your families are all invited. Richard can tell his tale then."

That night the Miller house rang with laughter and talk as

everyone gathered to celebrate Richard's safe return. They were happy for his parents, whom he had already visited in Boston, and they were glad he had come inland to Cincinnati.

A letter had been sent to the Millers that announced Richard's safe return, but Richard had arrived in Cincinnati before the letter. Everyone agreed that he would be safer if he lived away from the coastal harbors where the British were still kidnapping American young men, and they figured he could use his background in shipping to good advantage down by Cincinnati's docks.

The long table practically sagged under the weight of all the food. Everyone who came brought something to add to the meal. George thought that all his friends' pantries must surely have been emptied for this feast. He stuffed himself until he couldn't swallow another bite and couldn't move very comfortably, either. Like the others, he sat quietly, listening to the stories Richard told.

"The waiting was the hardest," Richard said. "I was knocked unconscious one night down by the harbor, and when I came to, I was on board a British naval ship. All I could think about was getting home. I protested that I was an American citizen, but the officers just laughed at me and told me to get to work, or else. We were so far out that land wasn't visible. I figured I was in the middle of the ocean with strangers who hated me, so escape wasn't really an option."

"Why did they hate you?" Betsy asked. She sat on a stool by the fire. Andrew sat next to her on the floor.

"They didn't even know you. How could they hate you?" George added.

"I was different." Richard shrugged. "Some of them actually believed I was a runaway British sailor who had been recaptured. They hated me for being a deserter. Others knew that I was an American. That was all they needed to know. The British still aren't very happy about American independence."

George listened as Richard told of the long years he had spent on British ships. Sometimes conditions had been decent, but often they had been terrible.

"I won't describe the conditions on some of those ships," Richard said. "Let's just say that none of God's creatures should ever be subjected to that kind of treatment. American sailors have much to be thankful for about the way American ships are run."

He paused as if silently reliving events he didn't want to explain. Silence filled the room. After a few minutes, Richard cleared his throat and continued talking. "Finally I just had to accept my plight and wait on God to deliver me. Along about then I decided that it wasn't so bad to be different, and I wasn't going to let those sailors change my mind. And then God sent help in a way I hadn't expected."

"What happened?" Betsy asked. George saw that her green eyes were bright with tears.

"It was an old salt of a seaman named O'Brien who helped me," Richard began. "He was an Irishman who had gone to sea many years before to flee from some kind of mess in Dublin. Of course most Englishmen think that the Irish are just short of barbarians, so he hadn't had an easy time of it on a British ship when he was younger. But I think he fought his way to some respect." Richard's face was solemn.

"In any case, his own experiences at being different hadn't softened his heart toward a displaced American. He was downright mean to me at times. In fact the only person he showed any kindness toward was the cabin boy, Harry. He was a sickly child who should never have been brought on board. O'Brien took a liking to the boy. Maybe the lad reminded him of the child he used to be. Myself, I just tried to stay out of O'Brien's way.

"Then I heard that the child was dying of a fever. But it wasn't just that. Seems that Harry was terrified of going to hell and kept begging for someone to help him. The man who told me about the situation said that O'Brien was almost as upset as the boy and would give anything to find a way to ease the boy's fears." Richard looked into the fire as he spoke.

"I wasn't sure what to do at first," he continued. "I wanted to talk to the boy, but O'Brien's dislike of me was well known. I was afraid he'd make a scene or do something worse if I showed up when he was already upset. But I went anyway. O'Brien just stood in the doorway of his cabin, frowning while I explained what I had heard and that I thought I could help. Without a single word he moved aside to let me in."

George watched Richard's face closely as the young man told how he had talked to young Harry about Jesus and heaven. The cabin boy had accepted Jesus as his Savior, and his fears had disappeared. Later that night, the young boy had died peacefully while Richard held one hand and the old sailor the other.

"Two nights later," Richard continued again, "I awakened to find my mouth gagged. Someone shoved me into a dinghy, rowed me to the Newfoundland shore, and then removed the gag. It was the Irishman. He'd gagged me to keep me from waking up anyone on board ship. Once we landed on Newfoundland, O'Brien threw me a small bag of food and rowed back toward the ship. And that is how I escaped, though it took me a while to make my way down to Boston again."

Questions flowed around George, but he was lost in thoughts of his American relative and the Irishman who had saved him. What would have happened to that dying cabin boy if Richard hadn't been there to answer his questions? Did O'Brien ever consider Richard's words about Jesus and become a Christian as well? George sighed. Some questions were destined to go unanswered in this world.

Soon the conversation slowed, and someone handed Betsy her violin and asked her to play. She just stroked the instrument's warm wood and looked at Richard with a smile. "Perhaps this violin should be played by its true owner."

Richard smiled. "Oh, I agree. And that's you."

Betsy hesitated but then slowly positioned the violin under her chin, held the bow in midair, and began to play.

George felt the floor beneath him quiver from a small tremor as Betsy played. It almost seemed that the earth was responding to the sweet strains of music that floated through the room. George's eyes prickled at the beauty of the old ballad that flowed over him. He was glad for the dim light.

Just when everyone seemed ready to weep, there was

another sound that was high pitched like the violin but considerably less musical. It was a dog howling. Jefferson, in fact, George realized. That dog never could listen to Betsy's violin without joining in. Everyone in the room laughed, including Betsy. In a moment she switched to a rollicking tune that soon had everyone clapping and singing.

George went outside to hush Jefferson. What a fine day it had been, he thought as he stood in the crisp night air. Richard was back safely, and the boat was almost finished. The day after tomorrow was Saturday, so they should have time then to get the rudders working. He could barely stand to wait that long.

Chapter Twelve
Finished at Last

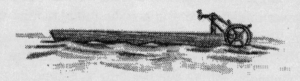

The next day began more quickly than even George could wish. He was awakened with a jolt to find himself on the floor by his bed. Confused and sleepy, he thought that he had somehow fallen out of bed like he used to do as a child.

Then he felt the now familiar rocking motion and realized Jefferson was nuzzling his face with his nose. Yet another earthquake, and it was a strong one if the plunging of the floor was any guide. George grabbed his shoes, trousers, and a blanket off his bed, called to Jefferson, and began the unsteady trek downstairs.

In the hallway he ran into Richard, who had spent the night with the Lankfords so he could go with George's father to the boatyard early in the morning.

"Come on," George yelled. "We'd better get outside."

Richard followed without a word. The pair hung onto the stair railing and partly crawled and partly walked down to the front hallway. The rest of George's family, including Jefferson, was right behind them. A particularly hard convulsion seemed to spit them all out the front door and onto the cold ground.

Once again they huddled together to wait for the worst to pass. Once again they prayed for God's mercy. To George it was almost sickeningly familiar. He had thought that he was over being afraid. That he could just trust in God and wait for whatever might come. But now he found that he was afraid again. Terribly afraid.

The noises of the earthquake surrounded him. He could hear chimneys falling and breaking glass and dogs howling and even a church bell ringing somewhere. His stomach lurched, and he felt sick.

Would it never end! George wanted to scream the words into the night. Why must they endure this yet again? Had God deserted them? He drew his legs up against his chest, wrapped his arms around them, and began to cry.

In a moment he felt an arm around his shoulders. He raised his face to see that it was Richard.

"Almost as bad as that hurricane I rode out last year on the ship," he hollered in George's ear. "Don't let it beat you."

The earth gave one last tremendous heave and quieted.

In the silence that came after the earthquake, George said,

"You're not afraid. How can you be so brave?"

"George, I'm scared silly," Richard freely admitted, "but you can't let fear rule you. Besides, I've learned lately that most of the time being brave is just doing what you know is right even when it isn't easy. So right now I tell my old knees to stop knocking and get me up and to work. God does the shoving, and somehow we get the job done."

George thought about Richard's words many times over the next couple days. They were miserable hours spent mostly outside as the earth trembled almost constantly. It was cold and wet, even with fires they built. No matter how many blankets they piled underneath them, the frozen ground chilled their bones as they tried to sleep.

But everyone was safe. The houses, although damaged, were still standing, and families and neighbors helped each other survive the terror. Eventually the tremors subsided, and once again normal life began.

After checking the summer kitchen to make sure that the boat had survived in one piece, George turned back to what seemed like a normal activity these days: cleaning up after a hard shake. It was commonplace to sweep up broken glass, crumbled mortar, and other fallen debris. Repairing the fissures in brick walls was a constant task. George did his share of work while he dreamed of finishing the boat. But at least the cleanup work gave him time to think about the rudders. He decided to use leather to make brackets to attach the rudder sticks to the rear of the boat. It wasn't fancy, but it should work.

One unexpected effect of the earthquake had been the

breakup of the ice on the Ohio. George had cringed Sunday afternoon when he first heard the cracking and popping, thinking it was another big shake coming just two days after the last. In a few moments he had realized that the noises were unaccompanied by the rolling ground of an earthquake. He raced to the river to see what was causing the unusual sound. Huge chunks of ice were tumbling in the current as the ice broke up. The river would be clear in a few days, especially if they had a warm spell.

That meant that the creek and mill pond should be clearing, too. It was getting closer to the time when they could safely launch the boat. If it was finished. George went back to his chores with renewed energy. There was no time to waste.

Two weeks later the boat was officially done. It had taken a week after the latest earthquake before the Lankfords and Lidells felt things had been cleaned up enough so that they could afford to let George and Charles return to work on the boat. In some ways, all the boys wanted to do was lie down and rest. They couldn't remember a time when they had worked so hard. But the thought of finally getting the boat finished gave them the extra energy they needed to keep going.

On a windy, cold Saturday afternoon in late February, Charles sat in the summer kitchen carving a name into the bow of the boat. "There." He leaned back to look at his handiwork. "It's done. What do you think?"

George looked up from where he was watching the pendulums quiver. "It looks great." He walked over to run his fingers over the carved word, *Cincinnati*. "I guess the boat's a she now that we've named her. I wonder why boats are always called she?"

"I don't know," Charles replied as he picked up some wood shavings from the floor, "but I've never heard one called he, that's for sure."

"I wish we could get her in the water today, but I know you're right. The weather needs to be better. It's just hard to wait. Seems I'd be used to that by now."

"At least we don't have to wait for news about the *New Orleans*," Charles said.

"We don't?"

"No, didn't I tell you?" Charles shook his head in disgust. "In the excitement of getting the boat finished, I plum forgot. A trapper came into the mercantile this morning with news about the steamboat. The Roosevelts were near the mouth of the Ohio River when the first earthquake struck, and they heard huge chunks of land break off from the shore and dump into the water.

"Terrified, they found a small island that they could moor by, and they waited out the night. Afterward, they couldn't recognize the river. The channels that the pilot depended on for deep water to travel in were filled with trees. Huge tree roots broke through the tops of the water. Needless to say, that slowed their progress considerably. And every time there was another aftershock, more damage appeared in the rivers. Somehow they made it down the Mississippi to Natchez by the end of January and were greeted by some mighty surprised people. Most folks had given up the steamboat as lost.

They couldn't imagine how it could possibly survive the upheaval in the rivers."

"That's a relief," George exclaimed. "I was worried about them. I guess they'll have some grand tales to tell when they get back up to Cincinnati later this year."

"I'll say," Charles agreed. "Now," he added, changing the subject, "is there anything else on the boat we could test without access to the water?"

The two boys checked over everything twice and concluded that anything on the boat that they could test on the crates in Mrs. Deering's summer kitchen, they had. Now the boat had to go in the water. If the weather cooperated, they would launch the next Saturday afternoon.

On Wednesday at school, Charles and George looked at each other in dismay. A cold spell was putting a fringe of ice back on the creek and mill pond.

"Wonder if this cold will last until Saturday," George said to Charles after school.

"I don't know," Charles replied, "but if it does, we'll have to postpone the launch again."

The boys stared at each other grimly.

Sure enough, when Saturday rolled around, the water was still frozen. The test run had to be put off until it warmed up a bit.

"So no launch today," Richard said as he pushed through the door of the summer kitchen.

"Not today," George said with a big sigh. "Too cold. The ice might clog up the paddle wheel, and then where'd we be?"

"You're right, but it's too bad," Richard said. He touched

the carved name on the bow. "The *Cincinnati*. A fine name for a good-looking boat."

"Thanks," Charles said. "George thought of it. Say, you're a boat builder now, too."

"Yes, and I'm enjoying being on solid ground for a change," Richard said.

"Not that the ground around here is too solid lately," George said.

Richard laughed. "You're right about that, but I like working for your father. Building boats is better than sailing on them for me right now."

"Who's sailing?" Betsy asked from the doorway. George looked up and saw that Emily was right behind his cousin. He wondered if she was towing any little brothers. If so, he'd better tie down the boat and stand guard. He relaxed when Emily pulled the door shut behind her without admitting any extra guests. Evidently she had found a way to escape her ever-present siblings.

"Well?" Betsy asked.

George turned his attention back to his cousin. "Well what?"

"Well who's sailing?" she repeated patiently.

"Nobody today," George answered glumly. "Especially not the *Cincinnati*."

"That's a shame," Betsy said, "but it is nasty outside. The boat looks grand, George."

"I still don't totally understand how it will work," Emily said. "Richard, you were explaining the drive mechanism to me the other day. Tell me some more about that." She smiled up at him and moved closer to the boat.

"I'd be glad to. Come back here and look at this." Richard motioned for Emily to join him in peering at the paddle wheel.

George rolled his eyes at Charles and went to stand in front of the fireplace. Lately Emily was terribly interested in Richard's opinion on every possible subject. And Richard seemed totally willing to talk at length in an effort to enlighten her. What was their problem?

Betsy grinned at George and shrugged her shoulders. The pair by the paddle wheel didn't notice the others' reactions since they were deep in discussion. George just shook his head. He had resigned himself to Andrew's attachment to Betsy, but now Richard was showing some of the same symptoms toward Emily. It was too much to take. He certainly hoped he would never behave in such a silly manner!

Time dragged by, one frigid day after another. At last the weather warmed, and a perfect Saturday dawned. George hurried through his chores. This was the day!

Franklin and Allie had been alerted since they had agreed to help carry the *Cincinnati* to the creek behind the mill pond. It took them ten minutes to maneuver the boat's awkward shape through the summer kitchen door. It was afternoon by the time the four boys arrived on the creek bank with the boat on their shoulders. They carefully lowered her to the ground near the water.

"Maybe we should put her directly into the mill pond," George said. "There's a lot more room to navigate."

"That's true," Charles said, "but if something goes wrong,

we can reach you and the *Cincinnati* more easily in the creek."

"Nothing will go wrong," George said with conviction. But he didn't argue. This was a test run, and he didn't relish taking an unplanned swim in the early March waters if it could be avoided.

"If she checks out, you can take her to the pond," Charles offered.

"Aye, aye, sir." George snapped a salute to Charles with a smile. Charles was like Betsy in one way: He was usually right, but he never rubbed it in.

"What's this I hear?" a new voice said from behind the boys. " 'Sir,' he says. Now doesn't that just beat all, Freddie?"

George looked up and groaned. The Jackson brothers were standing on the creek bank. He had wanted them to see his boat. After all, that was partly why he built it: so they would take notice of his work and want to be friends. But let them see her later, after the test. Later, when he could somehow get them to stop being mean to Charles. Right now he wished they would disappear. He knew they were only going to cause trouble. Why did they have to come to spoil his perfect day?

"Guess that means that old red man here is the captain of this ship," Ted said. "That seems mighty peculiar, George."

"Mighty peculiar," Freddie echoed. "I can't think why George here would let someone else be captain of his boat. Especially a freak like Charles."

George ignored the taunts. "Come on. Let's get this thing in the water." He motioned for the others to lift the boat so they could ease the *Cincinnati* into the creek. Franklin and Allie were at the front, while Charles guided the paddle wheel.

George watched the rudders. He had tied them up so they wouldn't catch on the weeds at the edge of the creek. He would untie them when they were ready to start. Gently the *Cincinnati* settled into the water.

"Of course with a boat like this contraption," Freddie continued, "perhaps the captain isn't important. Maybe he's supposed to go down with the ship."

"You're probably right," Ted agreed. "George must have dreamed this thing up in a nightmare." He nudged his brother and laughed. "It's sure to sink."

"Yeah, George. You and the captain will find yourselves swimming with the fishies." Freddie chuckled at his own humor.

"Now wait a minute." Charles threw down the tether rope he had been holding and started up the bank toward the Jackson twins. "George's boat will so work. You two don't know what you're talking about."

"Wow," Ted said. "The red man gets riled up. Do you think we're in danger? George, tell your friend to calm down."

"I should say so, George," Freddie agreed. "Tell your freaky friend to settle down. Maybe this so-called boat will work, but it isn't anything to get upset about." Freddie walked down and ran his hand over the side of the *Cincinnati,* which continued to bob slightly in the creek. "Actually you could bring it back to our workshop. We could help you fix it."

George felt like his body was stuck where he stood on the creek bank. But his mind wasn't stuck. It was spinning with thoughts. One word kept repeating: friend. Much as he had tried to deny it, Charles was his friend. Finally he knew what to do about the Jacksons. And there wasn't a moment to lose.

CHAPTER THIRTEEN
Settling the Score

It happened all in a rush. Suddenly George's feet were able to move again, and they carried him forward until he was nose to nose with Freddie. Anger swept over him like water over a waterfall, and it felt right.

"Listen, you two." George's voice was quiet and steady, but everyone knew he meant what he said. He raised his hand to point at Freddie and then Ted. "I've had enough. You're the freaks, not Charles."

"Now, George, don't get in such a state," Ted said.

"You're getting all excited over nothing," Freddie added.

"But it's not nothing." George shook his head. "You just don't get it."

"Maybe what we get is that you'd rather be friends with red man than us," Ted said.

George put his chin up and stepped closer. "Don't you ever call him that again."

He glared at Ted for a moment, and for once neither Jackson brother had anything to say.

"I'll grant that you've finally got something right," George told Ted, breaking the tense silence. "I would rather be friends with Charles than you two any day. He knows how to be a real friend. You two are just spineless bullies, looking for people to torment."

Ted backed up a step. He was frowning now. "There's no need to get so mean, George."

"Yeah, it was all in fun." Freddie joined his brother. "You just don't know how to take a joke."

"We aren't talking about jokes here. It wasn't funny to call Charles names, and it never will be." George stepped forward to close the gap between himself and the Jacksons again. "Maybe you Jackson brothers should go on home now while we get on with this boat launching."

Ted and Freddie exchanged looks and turned as one to leave.

"Oh," George called after them, "by the way, this is as much Charles's boat as it is mine." As the words left his lips, George knew that they were true. He couldn't have created this boat with its paddle wheel and rudder if it hadn't been for Charles.

George watched in silence as Ted and Freddie headed off toward town. Suddenly someone clapped him on the back. It was Allie. In the heat of the conversation, George had forgotten for a few moments that anyone else was near.

A sound from his other side made him whip his head around to see that Charles was standing there with Betsy and Emily. The girls must have arrived during his argument with the Jacksons.

"You were great," Allie said.

"Yeah, you said everything just right," Franklin said. "Those two always make me forget what I want to say."

Betsy stood in front of George and smiled. "Pretty brave, cousin." She nodded her head ever so slightly. "You know, that's what my mother would call righteous anger, and the Bible says sometimes it's necessary. Very necessary."

George looked at Betsy for a moment. Righteous anger. Brave. The surge of power he had felt when the Jackson twins left drained away until he felt empty and ashamed. He should have shown his righteous anger weeks ago. He sensed that Charles was standing beside him, but he dropped his eyes. He couldn't face his friend right now.

"George," Richard yelled from the path beside the creek bank a hundred feet downstream, "why is the *Cincinnati* going down the creek alone?"

George whirled around to see the boat floating down the creek toward the mill pond. They must have forgotten to tie it up after they put it in the water, and during the uproar, when everyone's attention was focused on the Jackson brothers, the boat had floated out into the current.

In seconds they were all scrambling down the bank toward the runaway craft. Just then Andrew came crashing through the brush on the creek bank near the boat. He splashed into the creek and grabbed the tether rope, which trailed from the bow of the *Cincinnati*. By the time George and Charles and the others arrived, Andrew and Richard had hauled the boat to shore.

"Thanks," George told Andrew and then Richard. "Thanks a lot. That was a close call."

"How did it get away from all of you, anyway?" Richard asked.

"Oh, we were watching George do a little righteous anger work," Betsy said. "I guess we were distracted." She just laughed at the puzzled look that passed between Andrew and Richard. "I'll tell you all about it later. Now, Andrew, you're very wet. Maybe you should go home and change."

George suppressed a strong urge to groan as Betsy fussed over Andrew, who stoutly proclaimed that he was just fine and was not going to let a little water make him miss the boat launching.

His comments made George's attention come back to the event they had been trying to get underway for what seemed like hours.

"Might as well set off from here," he said and looked at Charles, who nodded. "We know she's not going to sink right away."

They pulled the boat as close to shore as possible. There

was a big flat rock that would make a good place from which to climb into the hull.

"Get in, Charles," George ordered.

Charles looked confused for a moment. "What do you mean?"

"Get in the boat," George repeated. "She can't paddle herself, although she was doing a pretty good job a few minutes ago."

"But you're supposed to test it," Charles insisted.

"You can do it just as well. Go ahead." George motioned again. "Get in, Charles, before she decides to take off again."

"Are you sure?" Charles was frowning.

George nodded. "I'm sure. It's your boat, too. You go first."

Slowly a big grin spread across Charles's face. In a flash he climbed into the *Cincinnati* and settled on the wooden seat. He put his hands on the rudder sticks and his feet on the crank.

George held his breath as Charles began to slowly turn the crank. They had greased everything with lard, but there was still a lot of resistance. Charles was leaning back to get more leverage. Finally the paddle wheel began to turn ever so slowly, dipping into the water. The *Cincinnati* was launched! Her paddle wheel turned faster as Charles got the rhythm of cranking. On shore, everyone cheered.

In moments it seemed like the *Cincinnati* was racing toward the mill pond, and George ran beside her on the bank. He could barely keep up with the small craft, especially since he had to climb over dead trees and go up and around live ones that grew close to the water's edge. The others climbed back up the creek bank to the path and followed.

"George!" Charles yelled, distress in his voice.

George paused for a moment when he heard his name. Charles had stopped cranking, but the boat was still being carried by the current toward the pond. The creek had widened as it neared the pond, so Charles was well away from the bank.

"What's wrong?" George yelled. A frown had replaced Charles's usual smile.

"It won't steer," Charles shouted. "The rudders won't respond. Feels like they're stuck."

George thought for a moment. The *Cincinnati* was almost to the mill pond. There was a current there created by the water flowing toward the gates over the mill wheel, and the gates were probably wide open after the long spell of ice that had kept the mill from running. If he couldn't get the rudders to respond, Charles could always jump out, but the boat might crash into the gates if she couldn't be steered. Then they'd really have a mess. The boat could be destroyed.

George shook his head. He couldn't afford to panic. He had to think. What had gone wrong with the steering? Then George remembered, and he almost laughed with relief.

"Charles," he yelled. "I forgot to untie the rudders. The rope is there behind you." George watched as Charles twisted around in his seat. It seemed like a long time before Charles turned back around to give George a wave and begin cranking again.

The mill pond was dead ahead. The *Cincinnati* picked up speed as she emerged from the creek into the pond. George stood and watched anxiously. Would the rudders work? At last he saw that the boat was making a gradual arc as Charles steered her across the pond.

"She works! She really works!" George had to shout as he hurried back up the bank to go around the pond. She might not be sleek and steam-driven, but she was all theirs, and she worked.

A crowd had gathered at the edge of the pond nearest the mill by the time George arrived. Betsy and Emily led the cheering. He saw his parents and the Millers and Charles's parents. Mrs. Deering stood beside them, proud of her contribution to the event. Franklin and Allie jumped up and down and yelled directions to Charles. Richard and Andrew waved some kind of flags or maybe they were just feed sacks they had grabbed from the mill.

The crowd opened up to make way for George, and he was propelled to the water's edge. He joined in the cheers as Charles slowly circled the pond. At last Charles steered the *Cincinnati* directly toward the shore in front of George and the others. In a couple minutes, George reached out to grab the boat's bow. Charles climbed over the bow onto the ground.

Everyone talked at once. It seemed that they had all become experts and had plenty of ideas for improvements. George just laughed and agreed with every suggestion. Each person had to ask Charles what he thought. Was it fun? Was he scared? His answers were fast and excited, accompanied by a grin that was big even by Charles's standards.

Finally everyone started toward home. The sun was going down, and it was getting decidedly cooler. Mr. Edwards, who ran the mill, had said that the *Cincinnati* could remain tied up in the mill pond for the time being.

George and Charles were the last to leave. They checked and double-checked the ropes that tied their boat up to a tree on the bank. Having seen her escape once, they had no desire to return in the morning and discover that the boat had drifted off and crashed into the gates.

"I still can't understand how we let her get away from us earlier," Charles said.

"Me, either," George said, "but she won't get away this time." He tugged at the bow rope again.

They started down the road together.

"Charles." George knew that he had to talk to his friend about his encounter with the Jackson brothers, but what could he say? "Charles," he repeated and jammed his hands in his coat pockets. "I'm sorry. I should have confronted the Jackson boys a long time ago. It was wrong of me to let them go on acting that way to you without saying anything."

"That's all right," Charles said quietly. "I'm used to being teased, and you did a fine job today. They practically had their tails tucked between their legs when they left."

"I still should have done it sooner." George sighed.

"It doesn't matter, really." Charles stopped short. "I'm more concerned about our next invention. What should that be, do you think? Maybe we should go back to steam." He grinned at George.

"Great," George said. "You can tell my mother." A weight lifted as the two friends laughed together and started again for home.

There's More!

The American Adventure continues with *Trouble on the Ohio River.* Lucy Lankford desperately wants to learn how to play the piano and is counting the weeks and days until her new piano will arrive at the Cincinnati docks. Then the rains stop, the Ohio River dries up, and Cincinnati shuts down. Not only will Lucy's piano not be coming, but many people are thrown out of work and Lucy's best friend loses her house.

When Lucy isn't busy trying to figure out a way to get her hands on a piano, she and her cousin Ben Allerton are trying to solve the mystery of Raggy Wallace. Raggy lives on Sausage Row, down by the landing, and is always tormenting Ben. But for some unknown reason, Raggy treasures a worn scrap of flowered fabric. Why would a tough boy go to any length to protect such dainty material? As Lucy and Ben get to know Raggy, they think they may have figured out the answer and that Raggy may have more in common with Ben than anyone ever suspected.